Resting Place:
Phoenix

Resting Place: Phoenix

Mary Beasley

Get WRITE PUBLISHING

Edited by Pirkko O'Clock

ISBN: 978-1-945456-25-1 (sc)
ISBN: 978-0-9986604-3-1 (e)

Printed in the United States of America.

Come to me,
All you who labor and are heavy laden,
and I will give you rest.
Matthew 11:28

Dedications

This book is dedicated to My Heavenly Father, I called unto Him and He answered me!

To my children, Cody, Amber, Amir, Marcus, Britmarie, and Lewis who always asks for bedtime stories out of my head and caused me to dream big. You guys are my greatest treasure.

To Lewis, my husband and best friend, I am blessed beyond measure to have you in my life. Thank you for believing in me, for encouraging me and for always telling me, "Babe you can do it!" I truly could not have done this without you. 1-4-3

To Pirkko O'Clock, my editor, your red pen reminds me of the refiner's fire. I can't thank you enough for allowing God to use your gift to make my words flow.

Prologue

May 11, 2002

The sound of a door bell ringing invaded Sidney's dream of last night's prom date with J.P. Carter. The memory of it brought a smile to her lips. Groaning from the persistent ringing, she rolled over, peeping at the alarm clock that showed her in big block numbers that it was 6:30 in the morning. She groaned again and pulled the covers over her head, trying to ignore the offensive sound. After the fourth ring, she realized that she was the only one awake to hear the bell. Her brothers' bedrooms were in the basement, and with the basement door closed, they couldn't hear the ringing. Grams' room was on the back side of the house, and she was a sound sleeper. It annoyed Sidney that her room was at the front side of the house, and through her open window she could clearly hear that whoever was ringing the bell wasn't going away any time soon. Frustrated, Sidney threw off her covers and stomped her way to the window to see who could be visiting at this hour on a Saturday morning. She had already decided that if it was someone for Grams or one of her brothers, she was going back to bed, and they would have to wait until someone else answered the door or go away.

Pulling back the lavender curtain, Sidney couldn't contain the smile that crossed her face when she saw J.P.'s white Trans Am in the driveway. The car was a gift from J.P.'s father for his sixteenth birthday, and although she had ridden in it many times, she thought that it was a little too showy for J.P. However, after last night, her heart sped up just seeing his car. She hurriedly slipped on jeans and a tee-shirt and ran downstairs, pulling off her scarf, removing the rollers, and running her fingers through her hair before answering the door. Breathless, she opened the door saying, "I wasn't expecting you this ear. . . ." Her words froze as she looked into J.P.'s father's angry, brown eyes. Sidney just stood there staring for a few seconds before collecting her thoughts enough to ask, "Mr. Carter, what can we do for you? Grams is still asleep."

"I didn't come to see your grandmother. I came to see you." He stared at her with accusing eyes. "I know you've been seeing my son, and I'm here to stop it. You need to stick with your own kind and leave my son alone."

"Mr. Carter, J.P. and I are friends, and we did go out, but . . . ."

He snapped at her, "I don't want to hear it. I want you out of town and out of J.P.'s life, now. If you don't leave, I'll make you sorry; your whole family will suffer because you don't know how to stick to your own kind."

Fear begins clawing its way into Sidney's brain. With a shaky voice, she asked, "What are you talking about?"

Mr. Carter sneered at her, "Your grandmother is behind in her mortgage. I have a foreclosure notice right here. If you don't get out of town by Monday morning, I will file this notice and personally see to it that she loses this house and never owns property again in Resting Place."

Looking into Mr. Carter's intense, brown eyes, almost black in his determined stare, and then at the foreclosure paperwork in his hand, Sidney knew he was serious, and that he would foreclose on Grams' home. She wondered how Mr. Carter and J.P. could look so much alike and yet be so different. She knew J.P. loved her and Grams, but obviously, Mr. Carter didn't think she was good enough for J.P. Sidney's thoughts were racing. What could she do? She couldn't bear Grams losing her home because she was helping her brothers through college. After a long, agonizing pause, Sidney realized she had no choice, so she gave in, saying, "Okay, I'll leave for college right after graduation, and once I'm gone, I won't contact J.P."

Satisfied, Mr. Carter smiled and looked at Sidney and said, "I know John Paul thinks he cares for you, but believe me, it's just physical. You are a pretty, little thing. You two are from different worlds and have no future. You don't belong in his world and you never will."

His words cut deeply into Sidney's heart, but she held her head up and looked him in the eyes and said, "Mr. Carter, J.P. and I are friends. We always have been, and we always will be."

As he walked away, he said over his shoulder, "Not if I can help it, girl."

Sunday night, instead of picking out an outfit to wear to the graduation party, Sidney packed for college and cried for J.P. She knew that after the graduation ceremony, she wouldn't see him again, and the thought of it was like a knife through her heart. Praying for the strength to follow through for Grams' sake, and feeling an overwhelming desire to talk with J.P., she turned on her laptop and sent him one last e-mail. Hoping it would convey how much she loved him, she typed "J.P., I love you so much, and nothing will ever change that. Please wait for me." With a heavy heart, she hit the send button.

The next day, after Sidney graduated, she left Resting Place, leaving behind everyone and everything that she loved.

Chapter One

July 12, 2012

Tuesday morning, at 8:45 a.m. Sidney Weston walked off the elevator of the 25th floor of Bolen IT Company, heading to the morning meeting. She carried her laptop in her hand and wore a huge, uncontrollable smile on her face. Today she was dressed to impress in a new dark blue suit, with the skirt falling just above her knees, a light blue button-down silk blouse, and navy blue three-inch pumps. To top off her very professional appearance, Sidney wore her Akoya pearls, a gift from her grandmother for her twenty- seventh birthday. She had splurged on a new suit, wanting to look her best when she announced that she had attained the Burke Communication Company's account, the largest contract Bolen IT had every received. The excitement and anticipation she felt was almost more than she could stand.

Several junior executives had been competing to win the Burke account for a promotion to the executive level as well as the corner office. Today, for Sidney everything would change; she would not only be the youngest female to be promoted to the executive level, she would also be the first black female to be promoted to the executive level. As she walked into the meeting, she breathed a prayer of thanksgiving to God for blessing her and giving her favor with the Burke account. Then she whispered to herself, b*est day ever!*

The weekly staff meeting began as usual, with the junior executives reporting on accounts they had acquired over the course of the week. Sidney felt so excited, she didn't hear a word they said. When her turn to report came, she set up her laptop and passed out an outline of services Bolen would provide the Burke Company along with a letter of intent to sign with Bolen, naming Sidney Weston as the Contract Representative.

Sidney started her presentation and was on the second slide when Heather James, one of the junior executives who competed for the same account, stood up glaring at Sidney and said, "How did she get this account?" Not waiting for an answer, she continued, "That's my account and my promotion." She almost screamed as she turned to Roy Feeling, the President of Bolen IT. "Roy, you can't give it to her, anybody but her!"

Sidney looked from Mr. Feeling to Heather, realizing the meaning of her words. Fierce anger growing within her. She could hardly see straight. She clenched her fist, resisting the urge to slap Heather hard across the face. She reminded herself that as a Christian, she couldn't act on every impulse, even if the person deserved it. She took a deep breath instead and said, measuring her words, "As I recall, Mr. Feeling said that any junior executive who acquired the Burke Company account would also get a promotion to the executive level and the corner office in the executive suite. I believe the offer was for any junior executive, and as of today I have secured the Burke account."

Heather glared at Sidney, her green eyes fixed on her as she said in a hysterical voice, "You have nothing! You don't get it, do you? You walk around here thinking you're one of us. The truth is you will never get that promotion."

"That is enough, ladies," Roy Feeling interrupted. The 65-year-old President of Bolen IT looked from Sidney to Heather with intense, blue eyes that commanded respect and squashed any argument. As Sidney looked at him seated at the head of the conference table in his expensive, charcoal gray suit, she realized she was holding her breath, waiting, needing to hear what he had to say. After a long, uncomfortable silence, Roy cleared his throat and said, "Thank you, Sidney, good job." He then moved to the next agenda item, not allowing Sidney to finish her presentation. She looked at him stunned; the room returned to its normal quiet, and the next agenda item was discussed as if nothing great had even happened.

Sidney closed her laptop and took her seat as she pondered what just happened. She couldn't believe Mr. Feeling. *Shouldn't he offer congratulations or "great job" or something other than the next agenda item?* The Burke account was huge; Sidney envisioned them talking about how to transition the company and, of course, her promotion, *but the next agenda item! What was going on here?* She thought about last week's meeting when Heather expressed her frustration because her contact for the Burke Company had rescheduled with her for the third time. Everyone encouraged her, assured her that she would get the account and to keep at it. They even applauded her persistence, saying it was a critical element of leadership. *Even when Heather fails, she is applauded, but when Sidney succeeds, it's no big deal, good job, next agenda item.* She looked around the 10-foot mahogany conference table; the table that in the past brought them together as a team now became a barrier that separated her from everyone else. What did Heather mean? Was Sidney so naive that she didn't see that she wasn't accepted as the other junior executives were? Was she the token, meeting some requirement? What a fool she was to believe that she could advance on her skills, her achievements. As Heather's last statement became clearer, Sidney looked around the room to find that no one would make eye contact with her; they all seemed absorbed in their notes. Sidney's thoughts started racing so fast that she felt as if her head would explode, producing a massive headache. Then she got the message they were sending. In their silence, she heard it loud and clear. *We don't want you; you are not one of us, and you are not good enough for this job.*

Sidney took a deep breath and looked around the table again, realizing that she was the only African American in the room, and that was the problem; she was the problem. How many times had she heard that message before? That's why she had left home. No, not left, was forced to leave home, because she wasn't good enough. Those old feelings began to resurface. *I'm black, and I'm good, but not good enough.* Not good enough for J.P., not good enough for leadership, and certainly not good enough for this promotion.

Frustrated, angry and humiliated, Sidney made up her mind that she would speak with Mr. Feeling after the meeting. She didn't like confrontation, preferring to avoid it, but this was different. She needed to know where she stood with this company; she needed to challenge what she was seeing and hearing. She couldn't stay quiet and fade into the background. No matter how hard it would be, she had to question this.

When the meeting ended, Sidney made a beeline to her office to grab her notes from previous meetings, wanting to be prepared when she met with Mr. Feeling. She needed answers, and she had a bad feeling that once she received them, she wouldn't like what she heard.

While going through stacks of folders, Stephanie, her assistant, friend, and prayer partner stuck her head in the office, beaming and saying, "How was it? When do we move into the corner office of the executive suite?" Stephanie took one look at Sidney's face and said, "What happened?"

"I don't know, Steph. It was so weird; they were shocked into silence. Then Heather James jumped up and starting screaming at me, saying it was her account and her promotion, and that I would never get the promotion. She said it like she knew I wouldn't get it. We were arguing in the staff meeting, Mr. Feeling had to stop it."

"Wow that is weird. What did Mr. Feeling say?" Stephanie asked.

"Once he stopped us, he didn't say anything; he just moved on to the next agenda item. After the meeting, I think I saw someone consoling Heather. I need to talk with Mr. Feeling. I'm getting a bad feeling about this."

Stephanie closed Sidney's office door, walked over to her, and said, "Sidney, I overheard a conversation today between Judy in Contracting and her sister, Janie, in Payroll. I don't normally listen to other people's conversations, but I heard your name. Janie said that she thought it was so unfair that when you get a new contract and a promotion, all the other junior executives get promoted as well, but when one of the other junior executives receive a promotion everyone except you gets promoted." Stephanie saw the shocked expression on Sidney's face, walked over, gave her a hug, and said, "I don't like what I'm seeing."

"Stephanie, am I so blind that I couldn't see that they never wanted me?" Sidney said with tears forming in her eyes.

"No, they want you; you're too good at what you do. They just don't think you deserve more than the other executives because you're black. I'm sorry Sidney, I didn't see it either, but now that we know, let's pray for some direction before you talk with Mr. Feeling." Sidney just nodded her head as Stephanie began to pray.

≈≈≈

With notes in hand and a little breathless, Sidney headed for Mr. Feeling's office. Entering the executive suite, she noticed Fran, Mr. Feeling's assistant, was away from her desk, but his office door was ajar. Sidney walked over to the door, rehearsing what she would say, wondering if this was really a good idea. As she raised her hand to knock, she heard her name. Her hand stopped in mid-air. She listened as other members of the executive staff went back and forth, questioning how Sidney got the Burke account. Her heart broke as she heard them all agree that even though the Burke account would be Bolen's largest account, Sidney Weston just wasn't a good fit for an executive position. Sidney couldn't stop the tears from falling as she listened to how one of the board members had called to ask a favor of one of Burke's executives to meet with Heather, but he was out sick and couldn't meet with her. The question came up, "What other options do we have? We all know the promotion is no longer an option, not for Sidney." It was said with such disgust that it felt like someone had slapped Sidney. She had no idea that they felt so much hatred toward her. Not able to listen any longer, she turned to leave, wiping away tears as she ran into Roy Feeling.

He started to say something, but Sidney stilled his words when she looked into his intense, blue eyes, unable to hide her soul-deep hurt. Mr. Feeling looked at the open door and then at Sidney, realizing she had overheard the board members. Sidney watched while emotions left his face as he treated this event as casually as a rescheduled appointment. At that moment Sidney realized that he really did not care if she knew what they thought of her. He really thought it was okay to treat her like this. She just stared at him, it was like she was seeing him for the first time, and what she saw made her blood run cold. She tried to keep her voice from trembling, but failed, as she said, "I- I wanted to meet with you concerning the promotion, but- but I overheard that the promotion is no longer an option, because I got the Burke account." Sidney's voice grew stronger when she asked, "Is it because I'm too young, or a female, or because I'm black?"

Sidney waited for his response, taking note of him squaring his shoulders and looking past her as if she didn't matter at all, he said, "I can meet with you later today; check with Fran for an appointment time."

Realizing a meeting would not solve the problem she was seeing, Sidney said, "That won't be necessary, sir. I see that I am not wanted in this company; you will have my resignation on your desk by close of business."

Chapter Two

Sidney listened as the phone rang at Martha Rose's house in Resting Place, Maryland, praying that her grandmother would pick up, needing her to make the pain and hurt go away as she'd done countless times over the years. After the fourth ring, her grandmother picked up, "Hello."

"Grams, hi; it's Sidney."

"Hi, baby, what's wrong?" Martha Rose asked, hearing Sidney's despondent voice.

"I quit my job today." Sidney could hardly believe she was saying those words as she held the phone to her ear.

"What?" Her grandmother asked with concern in her voice. "I thought whoever got the Burke Company account would be promoted to the executive level."

"Grams, it wasn't real, at least not for me. They never thought I could get the account. They wanted someone else, someone better suited for the job."

"Girl, what are you talking about? You worked hard to get that account; you put your heart and soul into that company. Who else could be better suited for that promotion?" Grams voice was getting louder, indicating her level of anger concerning what she was hearing.

"Grams, they want someone white. I overheard the executives talking about how even though the Burke account is the largest they have ever got, the promotion isn't an option for me. They said I wasn't a good fit." Sidney took a deep, painful breath and told her grandmother of the morning meeting, what she overheard outside Mr. Feeling's office and finally, her conversation with Mr. Feeling. "Grams, while I was sitting in the morning meeting, I felt like I had stepped back in time to a place where it was against the law to look them in their eyes or share the same water fountain. I know I can't stay here, but I don't know what to do now."

Martha Rose's words were compassionate and seasoned with prayer. Sidney could picture Grams' gentle smile, her kind, hazel eyes and long, black hair with streaks of gray. Over the years, Sidney had come to realize how blessed she was to have a praying grandmother, and she ran to her in times of stress. "Sidney, I know you're disappointed. You worked hard for that

18

promotion, and I know you're angry and frustrated right now. However, I also know that this day did not catch God by surprise. He has a plan for you, and I know that He will work this out for your good. Why don't you come home? You can get a fresh start and see what God wants you to do next."

Sidney had been thinking a lot about Resting Place, longing to be someplace where she did fit in. If she had her way, she would never have left, but it wasn't her choice then. Now maybe it was time to go home. "Okay, Grams, I'll clear out here and start making plans to move home."

Hanging the phone up, Sidney noticed Stephanie standing in her office. "I was eavesdropping," she said with no sign of guilt. "So when will we leave for Resting Place?"

"Steph, I can't ask you to quit your job."

"You didn't ask, and let me make myself clear; you are not leaving me here. I'm going with you. So call Grams, and let her know that her two girls are coming home."

Sidney walked around her desk and gave Stephanie a big hug, thanking God for this woman who was more like a sister than a friend. They had been through a lot together over the past five years. Stephanie had been assigned as Sidney's assistant when she first started at Bolen IT as a junior executive. Stephanie had a reputation of coming in late for work and taking frequent breaks. Sidney had prayed about how to approach Stephanie's performance issues before scheduling a meeting with her. Three weeks of tardiness and having to seek her out several times during the day caused Sidney to make a decision to do something about it. While praying about what to say to Stephanie, the Lord impressed upon Sidney the Scripture, *Now we who are strong ought to bear the weaknesses of those without strength and not just please ourselves. Romans 15:1.*

With Stephanie in her office, Sidney silently prayed for wisdom and for words that would help and not do harm. "Stephanie, I don't know what's going on, but I want to help."

Sidney's words were so sincere and kind that they caused Stephanie to release a burden that until that day she had carried alone. Stephanie cried as she told Sidney about her terminally ill mother; how she couldn't lose her job because she was their only support. She talked about her fears because her mother had so little time left. As she poured out her heart to Sidney, peace settled in Stephanie's soul and a bond formed between them.

Sidney shared God's love and His plan of salvation with Stephanie as she pulled out a Bible from her desk drawer. She showed Stephanie Scripture after Scripture of God's love, forgiveness and salvation. Stephanie absorbed each Scripture as if they were cool water to her thirsty soul. She asked question after question; her smile becoming brighter as hope blossomed in her heart. With tears streaming down Stephanie's face, Sidney led her to the Lord and welcomed her to the Body of Christ. They hugged and cried and thanked God for His grace. The following Sunday, Stephanie visited and joined Sidney's church, Christ International Church, (CIC). Stephanie was accepted into the congregation with open arms. As she settled in with her new church family, she began to open up and accept the love they freely gave. She was overwhelmed by the support and fellowship they provided to her and her mother. Before Stephanie joined CIC, her mom never had visitors. After joining, women from the church visited her mother almost every day. They came to clean, cook, or just sit and talk with her. These women gave Stacey Reed something that she hadn't had in years; friendship, and Stephanie thanked God every day for that precious gift. A month after joining CIC, Stephanie led her mother to Christ. After accepting Jesus Christ as her Savior, a peace entered Stacey Reed that remained with her until the day she died. Stephanie truly understood the Scripture that asks, *death, where is your sting?* Never had she felt such peace, and even joy, knowing that when her mother closed her eyes in this life, she would open them in the presence of the Lord.

Stephanie became one of the best executive assistants at Bolen IT. Many offices and other agencies approached her with offers of new jobs and promotions. Her skills were excellent, and Sidney knew that Stephanie could work anywhere. Whenever she was presented with a new job offer, Stephanie turned them down, stating that she was not interested. Sidney had talked with Stephanie and tried to encourage her to advance in her career, not wanting to hold her back. Stephanie had responded, "It's not about the money or the position. You believed in me, and were there for me when I had no one. I will always be grateful, and will always do my best for you."

Now, they shared tears and a hug. Sidney said, "Okay, we'd better make plans if we're moving to Resting Place."

"Give me 30 minutes to cancel your appointments and type up our resignations, and then we can make plans to move." With a big smile and tears still wet on her face, Stephanie darted out of the office with her blond ponytail bouncing behind her.

Sitting at her desk, Sidney considered her relationship with Stephanie. Sidney didn't have a sister, being the only girl with three brothers, but whenever she thought about a sister, Steph's face came up. They were so different; Stephanie was barely five feet tall, with long, blond hair and creamy, ivory skin, versus Sidney's five-foot eight inches, long, black hair, and pecan brown skin. They were as different as night and day, but their bond was unbreakable. Sidney decided at that moment to ask Stephanie to be her partner with West Tech, the small business she had started to create jobs for some of their church members who had IT experience. Feeling peace seeping into her soul, Sidney prayed. *Thank you Lord for my sister, Stephanie, and thank you that I am not alone on this journey home.*

Chapter Three

At the close of business, Sidney walked to Mr. Feeling's office with her resignation letter in hand. She, found herself wondering how she had missed it for so long, why hadn't she seen that she was treated differently? Then it dawned on her that every time she was promoted for an account she secured, the other junior executives were advanced along with her. She was told it was a team effort, however, she was not included as part of the team in their promotions. That was a subtle reality that she had never noticed. Now she could see that despite her team efforts, she was the lowest-paid junior executive. Sidney also realized that all the others called Mr. Feeling by his first name, Roy, but she had not been given permission to do the same. Now that her eyes were opened, she could see and understand a lot. How subtly they used her, and how foolish she had been for thinking she was accepted. She waited for the anger, and even hatred, to come towards these people, but the only thing she felt was the need to separate herself from them as quickly as possible.

As Sidney walked past the conference room, she thought about the events of the day. She came in thinking she was going to get a promotion, and now leaving work, she was handing in her resignation. Of course, she knew that none of the events of the day had caught God by surprise, but she couldn't help questioning why He let her get the Burke account if He knew she was going to end up quitting her job. She breathed a comment, *I don't get it, God. I don't understand.*

When Sidney walked into the executive suite for the second time that day, Fran had left for home, and again Mr. Feeling's office door was open. She knocked before entering.

"Sidney, what can I do for you?" He spoke as if nothing had happened.

"I am submitting my letter of resignation, sir." She handed him the letter. For a few seconds, he just looked at her as if he couldn't believe she was serious.

Taking the letter, he said, "Sidney, you do good work, and granted, the Burke account is one of our largest accounts to date. I would be willing to give you a salary increase for getting the account."

As Sidney listened to him, she got the impression that she should be grateful that he had offered her a raise, as if that would make it all better. "That is a generous offer, sir; however, I have already accepted another offer." She did not say that the other offer was from her grandmother to come home. "I hope to have all of my current accounts transferred within the next two weeks. Goodnight, Mr. Feeling." Not giving him time to say anything else, she left his office.

Roy Feeling read through Sidney's resignation letter. Then sat back in his chair and thought about what had happened that day. He admitted that things could have been handled better. Signing off on Sidney's letter and routing it to Human Resources, he felt a cold chill come over him. Roy knew it was a mistake to let Sidney go, but he also knew that he would never give that young, black woman a senior executive position.

Walking back to her office, Sidney started processing all the work needed to close out her desk, making mental notes about who could handle each account. She felt a little guilty about leaving her clients on such short notice. The relationships she had developed with each account were excellent; she knew her clients trusted her and counted on her support, and she gladly went the extra mile for them. Grams always used to say, "Give your all in everything you do, and do everything with excellence!" Sidney applied that principle with every account and every project. Whenever she secured an account, she considered it a new assignment from God; therefore, she served her clients as unto the Lord. She loved her job and would miss it and her friends and clients, but she knew she couldn't stay. Once she made the decision to return home, it just felt right. She had a peace about it that made leaving Bolen easier.

When Sidney entered her office, she could see Stephanie clearing out some files. She picked up the phone to make reservations at Stephanie's favorite restaurant, so they could plan their trip back to Resting Place. Hanging up, Sidney booted up her computer to email her clients, notifying them of her departure from Bolen IT. Thanking them for allowing her to serve them, she informed them that their accounts would be assigned to other junior executives. As she finished typing each e-mail, she copied the executive board and her fellow junior executives. Before she hit the send button, she prayed that her clients would be well cared for, especially the small minority businesses.

≈≈≈

Once the news was out about Sidney's departure from Bolen, a steady stream of visitors started stopping by. Some came to wish her well, some to be nosey, while others came to see why she was leaving. Among those who wanted to know why was Laura Burke of the Burke Company. One week after Sidney handed in her resignation, while preparing an account for transfer, the phone rang. Sidney answered, "Bolen IT, Sidney Weston. How may I help you?"

"Hello, Sidney, this is Laura Burke. May I have a moment of your time?" Laura spoke in a strong, alto voice with a slight British accent.

Sidney knew she would hear from Laura, and had tried unsuccessfully several times to meet with her personally over the past week in her office or at their church. Laura, a long-time member of Christ International Church, (CIC) worked with the Welcome Committee and was one of the first people Sidney met when she joined. While talking with Sidney about what she would like to do at CIC, Laura offered to mentor her. After six months at the church, Sidney shared with Laura her dream of starting an IT help desk business. With Laura's assistance, connections and guidance, Sidney launched West Tech six months later. Laura was not only her mentor; she was also a cherished friend. Sidney responded to the familiar voice, "Hello, Laura, I'm sorry I didn't get a chance to talk with you sooner about leaving Bolen. Your schedule has been really full."

"Yes, it has, and I'll be leaving in the next few days, flying home to England. I'll be visiting family and will be gone for a month, but before I leave I wanted to find out why you're leaving Bolen. I have heard the politically correct answer; now I want to know the truth. And Sidney, before you answer, remember we are sisters in Christ first, then friends, and then business associates. I know you love your job and with my business account, you are a valuable asset to Bolen. So, why are you leaving?"

Laura's no-nonsense approach to business and life had enabled her to take over a failing family business and turn it into one of the leading communications companies in the industry. Laura weighed about 105 pounds, was five feet tall and in her mid-forties, but could stand toe to toe with any of her male counterparts, and on many occasions made them back down. She was a force to be reckoned with in the business world, and today Sidney understood why, as she told Laura about the, expected promotion, the meeting, what she had overheard and finally, her last conversation with Mr. Feeling. Sidney also shared about relocating to Resting Place, and focusing on growing West Tech there.

There was a long pause before Laura spoke, her British accent a little more pronounced, "Sidney, I'm very sorry you had to go through that, and I am really glad you quit. I have a lot to say about what you've just shared with me, but I've learned over the years that actions speak louder than words. I will withdraw my intent to sign with Bolen IT. I would like to have West Tech service my company, but I know you're not big enough to support us. Do you think you could partner with another larger company within the next 30 days?"

Sidney looked at the phone, stunned. "Are you serious?"

"Of course I'm serious. The only reason I signed with Bolen was because I wanted you, Sidney. I know the quality of your work and your work ethic. I trust you, and I trust your judgment. So, find a company; use our account as leverage with your proposals." After a pause, Laura continued, "You, not good enough? Huh, well we will see about that."

Joy started bubbling up inside Sidney as she replied, "Laura, thank you so much! I will do my best for you. It means a lot to me that you would trust me with your account." They talked for another 30 minutes about the details. Sidney mentioned that Stephanie was leaving Bolen as well and had agreed to become her business partner. She also told Laura that they were changing the business name to from West Tech to Phoenix. Sidney could hear the pride in Laura voice as she excitedly said, "Bravo Sidney! You and Stephanie make an excellent team! I'm very proud of you, and Phoenix is such an appropriate name. Now if I can give you a little advice," Laura's voice became all business. You need to contact your current clients and inform them of the change and request recommendations under your new business name. Your business is young, but it is not brand new, and the letters of recommendation will help you present as an established business." Sidney thanked her and made a note to have Stephanie contact their clients. Laura informed Sidney that her secretary would have a letter of intent to sign with Phoenix drawn up and sent to her home in the next day or two. When Sidney hung up the phone she sat at her desk, thanking God for the gift of the Burke account. *Wow, God, I understand now. Thank you, Father.* Grinning, she jumped up and ran to Stephanie's office to tell her the wonderful news.

After three weeks of non-stop work and packing, transferring accounts, researching potential parent companies, and giving away anything they could, Sidney and Stephanie were exhausted but ready to move on. Sidney marveled again at how easy it was to hand in her resignation and close out her office. She considered the peace she felt to be a sign from God that it was time to go.

Thinking over the past years, Sidney realized that she and Stephanie could use everything they had learned from working with Bolen IT to grow Phoenix. Once she understood that she would never hold an executive position at Bolen, leaving wasn't a problem. The bottom line was that she was good at her job, even great, but just not the right color; she wasn't white. Mr. Feeling didn't come right out and say that. He said she wasn't a *good fit* for that position, but she knew exactly what he meant. His opinion of her hurt deeply, bringing back memories of rejection that she thought she had gotten past. Hearing his code words, "not a good fit," in other words, "not one of us, not white," opened old wounds too painful to face.

There were only two things Sidney had worked extremely hard to accomplish, and each time she had done the work and met the requirements, the prize had been snatched away. One was the senior executive position, and the other was a future with J.P. Carter. All because she wasn't considered good enough; she wasn't white.

Friday morning, Sidney and Stephanie stopped at the security desk and turned in their ID badges before leaving Bolen for the last time. Sidney felt free and ready for whatever plans the Lord had for her. As they headed out of New York City in her red Subaru Forester, Stephanie began praying that God would give them safe travels and guidance concerning their partnership with Phoenix, asking God to bless their small business and give them wisdom about how to grow it. Sidney echoed her amen to close the prayer.

Chapter Four

Three hours into their drive Stephanie turned the music down and asked the question that Sidney had been avoiding ever since she had decided to move home. "Sid, what about J.P.?"

"What about him?" Sidney said, trying to sound unconcerned.

Stephanie stared at her best friend and said, "Who are you kidding? I was there when you got the wedding invitation. I cried with you, prayed with you, and watched you mourn J.P. Carter. Don't kid yourself, Sidney. You still care about that man, and it's going to be hard seeing him again. You need to think about how you're going to deal with it."

After a long silence, Stephanie spoke again, "Sidney, you're going to see him! It's not like the times we visited for a day or two. How are you going to deal with seeing him again?"

Sidney shook her head and said in a slow, measured voice, "I don't know, Steph. I don't know. He's married. I can't do anything about that. I'm praying about it. God promises not to put more on us then we can bear. I know He won't make me ashamed, and He is gracious. I have to trust Him with this. I really don't have a choice. I just have to trust Him."

Stephanie leaned over and patted Sidney's hand on the steering wheel and said, "I know it won't be easy, but I'll be there to help or give a shoulder to cry on. I'll be there."

Unable to voice the gratitude in her heart, Sidney smiled and nodded her head. Understanding, Stephanie returned her smile, and they fell into a comfortable silence as they continued to draw near to their unknown destiny, trusting God for what they could not see.

≈≈≈

As they drew nearer to Resting Place, Sidney's thoughts drifted back to J.P. Ten years had passed since she left, though she had sometimes visited for a day or two, just to check on Grams and see her brothers for a few hours. She hadn't dared stay longer for fear of seeing J.P., or worse J.P.'s father.

When she joined CIC, Sidney had to face the wounds she carried with her from Resting Place. That was a long, painful journey that she continued to thank God for. She marveled at the patience of the Holy Spirit. In His gentle way He worked with her to move beyond her anger, hurt and pride, to reach a place of forgiveness. Next to leaving Resting Place, it was the hardest thing she had ever done, but today she knew in her heart she had forgiven Mr. Carter for forcing her to leave J.P. She also forgave J.P. for not waiting for her, realizing no relationship could last without any contact. Then she had to repent again for hating Mr. Carter for forcing her to leave Resting Place. The forgiveness process took a few years, and she had to see her part in it as well. Sidney admitted her faults; she realized she could have contacted J.P. when she received the e-mail about his engagement or the invitation to his wedding, but she let pride and insecurity get in the way. It felt good to be free of the anger and hurt; now the only thing that remained was the love she held for J.P. The love endured no matter how hard she tried to fall in love with someone else; she just couldn't make herself feel anything close to the love she shared with J.P. She was sick of herself and angry with her treacherous heart for still loving J.P. Many days she berated herself, *Why can't you move on? The man is married! What is wrong with you?* It was as if she didn't possess her own heart to give to another. Many, many nights she prayed, begging the Lord to remove the love she held for J.P., to no avail. It was hard enough living in New York, comparing every guy she met with J.P., and having them come up short because they weren't J.P.

Since making the decision to go home, thoughts and memories of J.P. constantly flooded Sidney's mind. She could resist those thoughts during the day, pushing them away whenever they drifted through her mind, but the dreams at night were impossible to control. For three weeks she dreamed about their conversations, times they spent together, their first kiss, their last kiss, the secret codes they used when other people were around. When morning came, Sidney couldn't help mourning what was now lost.

Now just the thought of living in Resting Place, seeing him happy with his wife and family caused Sidney to panic, making her plead more urgently for the Lord to remove the feelings she had for that man. *Lord, I can't watch him with his wife and children, knowing that if things had been different, it would have been me. Dear Lord, please help me.* Nothing; the heavens stood silent, not a word from God's throne of grace. Shaking off the memories, Sidney said with resolve, *Lord, I don't understand what You are doing here, but I want to bring You glory wherever I am, even if it hurts. I trust*

You, Lord; I'm not sure that I trust me, so forgive me when I mess up, try me again.

Chapter Five

J.P., Board President, ran his fingers through his thick, curly, brown hair, a habit he had when he was tired. He looked around the conference room table at the Technology Club Help Desk Crew (TCHD) Board of Directors, minus one, Sidney. "Okay this is the last proposal, a company called Phoenix. Does anyone have feedback on this one?"

Larry Payne, the Web Developer, spoke up, "I like this company; they propose to target major companies in the New York, New Jersey area. The companies we currently contract with are in the southern regions. We can expand our reach, open more satellite offices, and create new jobs. It looks like a win-win situation."

Marcus Weston, Sidney's twin brother, J.P.'s partner, Vice President of the Board and the Computer Hardware Manager, said, "This proposal offers the greatest benefit because they are bringing a major company with them. The Burke Company is an established family-owned business in New York City. If this works out, we could also promote some of our current staff to head up a few satellite offices. I like it as well, and think it's definitely worth considering."

J.P. spoke up, "I also like the company, and our goals seem to be similar. I've done some background work on Phoenix; there's not a lot of information on the owners, but the company was established eight years ago and worked through local churches, several schools and some colleges in the area, and it's a female owned company. They have excellent references from the schools and colleges. It seems like a big jump from a local school to the Burke Company, but then again, we started in the school system, too."

Peggy Neil, Software Manager, asked, "So far I see how we can benefit, but why join us? What's in it for them?"

J.P. answered, "I think they need us or a larger company to handle the Burke Company. Phoenix is small; I don't think they could support a business the size of Burke on their own. They're also asking that some of the satellite offices be opened near the church where they were established and the surrounding area. They want us to guarantee that Phoenix's current employees retain their jobs and pay, and they are also asking for board membership." The room grew silent after J.P.'s last statement. They had determined long ago that only the TCHD original team and their families would hold membership on the board.

Marcus said, "We can all agree that this company can benefit us, and we can all accept the first two conditions, but we are not prepared to open membership to the board. With that said, I also think both sides can benefit from a merge. If they need us to help manage the Burke account maybe we can negotiate about membership to the board? Do we know how firm they are about the membership issue? Can we meet in person and talk about it?"

J.P. replied, "The point of contact is a woman named Stephanie Reed; I believe she's a partner in Phoenix. Marcus, can you have your assistant give her a call and arrange a meeting for next week? If we can work around the membership issue, I think we can do business."

Marcus smiled and said, "I agree. Is everyone available next Wednesday at 10:00 a.m.?" There was a pause while the board members checked their schedules. Everyone confirmed availability for the following Wednesday, then the meeting was adjourned.

≈≈≈

As the two of them headed back to their offices, J.P. asked Marcus what he thought about the merger. J.P. valued his friend's opinion and trusted his judgment. Having gone through a lot together over the last ten years, J.P. had learned to allow Marcus to speak into his life, although sometimes what Marcus told him was really hard to hear. He knew Marcus cared enough to address the hard issues and his heart issues. J.P. turned to Marcus when Sidney left, talking out his feelings while playing one-on-one basketball to work off his anger and frustrations. He remembered Marcus calling him in the middle of the night to check on him. Marcus always seemed to know whenever things got bad. Even though J.P. knew Marcus was as lost as he was when Sidney left, he was a source of comfort and strength that J.P. desperately needed.

It was this relationship that caused J.P. to ask Marcus to be his partner with the TCHD Company. J.P. considered that to be the best decision he could have made when he found out he had an inheritance from his mother. On his twenty-first birthday he received a letter from her, telling him she wanted him to use the money to follow his dreams. J.P. knew exactly what he wanted; he had been saving to start a computer help desk company. It was his and Sidney's dream ever since their high school computer project. After praying and discussing it with Marcus, J.P. and he formed the TCHD Company. Looking back over the years, J.P. could never have predicted the success they experienced. Over the past five years TCHD had moved from having a few contracts and holding their own to discussing mergers to help smaller companies. He remembered Sidney talking about establishing their company and then becoming a bridge for other companies to get started. Every time he considered a merger, the process was bittersweet because Sidney wasn't there to share their dream come true.

It still amazed J.P. how easily his thoughts often wandered to Sidney. He had resisted thinking about her for years, not wanting the feel the loss and anger that accompanied memories of her. When Sidney left, it crushed J.P. on many levels; she was his best friend, his partner with the Technology Club Help Desk project, and the love of his life. He mourned the loss and longed for their friendship and the love he knew they shared. He tried to tell himself that they were kids experiencing puppy love, and what they had would fade with time. Ten years later his feelings for her endured. He knew what they shared was special and wondered if Sidney even thought about him as he couldn't help thinking about her.

"Hey, are you coming over tonight?" Marcus asked. "Grams said she's been thinking about you and wants to see you."

Smiling at the thought of Grams thinking about him, J.P. said, "My dad is having a party at the house for the bank staff and wants me to stop by. I think he's still trying to fix me up. Tell Grams I'll be a little late, but I'll be there."

"Great, maybe we can shoot some hoops before it gets too dark."

"Sounds like a plan. Tell Kevin and Tate to get ready to sweat."

"Will do."

Changing the subject, J.P. asked, "What's your gut feeling about this Phoenix proposal?"

"The proposal looks great, but I have the feeling that there is more to this than what we see, and it may bring some unexpected changes."

"I get that, too, but I'm not sure that it's a bad thing." J.P. said.

"Well, it's definitely worth praying about." While the rest of the TCHD Crew left for home, Marcus and J.P. joined hands and asked God for wisdom and direction concerning the Phoenix proposal.

Chapter Six

The party was in full swing when J.P. arrived at his father's house. He sat in his truck, dreading going in and pretending to have a good time when all he really wanted to do was go to Grams' house, where he where he could relax and enjoy being with friends. He hated his father's parties, which always ended up being matchmaking events, and he purposed in his heart not to be a part of any more of his father's plans to find him a girlfriend. Breathing a heavy sigh, J.P. stepped out of his truck, checked his appearance in the side view mirror, and walked into the house, greeting his dad. "Hello, Father."

"Aw, John Paul, you made it! It's good to see you, son. Everyone, you all remember John Paul, my son?" Several people came over to greet J.P., along with a few single women.

J.P. leaned close to his father and said, "Dad, please don't try to fix me up again. I'm not going to go along with it this time."

"John Paul, I'm not trying anything, just relax and enjoy the party, and if one of these lovely women catches your eye, all the better."

"Okay, Dad, but I have a late meeting tonight, so I can only stay for an hour." J.P. could see his father was upset at his plans, but made no other comment as he faded into the crowd of people, making casual conversation. J.P. began working the room, a talent he had picked up over the years to ensure he was seen by everyone and to show his dad that he did indeed mingle with his guests.

While making his rounds, J.P. was approached by several young women who expressed interest in dating him. Some dropped hints, some were very bold, and then there were the ones who offered a good time with no strings attached. They were all very beautiful women, and he knew they were the type who appealed to his dad and had been appealing to him for a long time, even before his mother died. J.P. didn't understand at the age of seven, but at twenty-seven, he understood his parents' arguments, the sadness in his mother's eyes, and the tears she tried to hide from him when his dad didn't come home or when a sudden urgent business trip came up. J.P. often wondered if his mom would have lived longer or been happier during her last years if his dad had really loved her. Once he understood their loveless marriage, he was determined that his own life would not be a reflection of his dad's life. When he married, it would be because he loved the woman with all his heart and it would be for life.

≈≈≈

Making polite excuses, J.P. moved to the next group of people. He told himself to stick to the plan, and in about twenty minutes he would be a free man.

"John Paul! There you are; I've been looking for you."

J.P.'s spine stiffened as he reminded himself that his dad didn't play fair. Turning, he said, "Melinda, how are you?" Melinda was beautiful, tall and blond, with big, blue eyes. Any man would have loved to date her and even marry her, but J.P. was never attracted to her. She was one of his father's arranged dates, and she was a little too aggressive for him. Melinda was a woman on a mission, and from the way she was looking at J.P. he was her latest assignment.

"John Paul, why haven't you called me? Don't tell me you're still upset over that little rumor?"

Little! That rumor had people coming out of the woodwork, congratulating him; even his clients had heard about it and were calling and sending cards. It took a great deal of effort to clear up that rumor, and

J.P. vowed he would not open that can of worms again. "I've been really busy, Melinda."

"Don't be upset J.P.; I thought it was sweet, even prophetic."

J.P. looked at Melinda, wondering if she actually considered the two of them to be in a relationship. He had never indicated anything serious between them. He had only shared a meal with her, one meal. Thinking fast, he gave her a smile and said, "Melinda, you flatter me, but we both know I am way out of your league. I couldn't measure up, and I wouldn't even try." Before she could answer he looked at his watch and said," Excuse me Melinda, I promised Mrs. Fields I would stop by her table before I leave."

Melinda touched his arm, leaned forward, turned her big, blue eyes on him, gave him a sensual smile and said, "You never know, J.P., we could be great together."

Looking into her eyes, J.P. realized again how senseless it was to even try to date anyone. With what Melinda was offering with those stunning, blue eyes, most men would be putty in her hands right now, but J.P. couldn't get Sidney's warm, brown eyes out of his mind. She had spoiled him and made him immune to the invitation Melinda offered. Looking over her shoulder, he saw Mrs. Fields and said, "Excuse me, there's Mrs. Fields. I need to catch her before I leave. Nice talking with you, Melinda." J.P. left her standing, staring at him as he made a beeline for Mrs. Fields' table and putting a safe distance between them.

Melinda hid her frustration with a smile as she thought about all she had been promised by John Carter Sr. if she married J.P. Carter. When she had been approached with this proposal, she had thought it would be easy. However, J.P. was hard to seduce, but she would not give up. The prize of being Mrs. J.P. Carter and all it included was too great to let go.

≈≈≈

Twenty minutes later J.P. was in his truck, beating a hasty path to Martha Rose's house with a smile on his face and a basketball game in sight. He said a prayer of thanks to God for getting him out without another encounter with Melinda. J.P. knew that his dad was encouraging Melinda to pursue him and made up his mind to talk with him about it. He might never see Sidney again, but he would not settle for and marry someone he didn't love.

Parking in Grams' driveway, J.P. hopped out of his truck, grabbed his gym bag, and headed to Marcus' room to change clothes. Once he had done that, he went to the kitchen to find Grams.

As he entered, he came up behind her, enfolding her in a big bear hug. "Hi, Grams how are you?" he whispered in her ear.

"Hi, baby, I'm fine. I'm so glad you came; I've been missing you."

"I've missed you, too, Grams. I've been really busy, but you know I can't stay away from my favorite girl."

His comment made her blush. Smiling, she said, "You do my heart good, boy. I love you."

"I love you, too, Grams."

"Now get out of my kitchen; the boys are out back."

Grinning from ear to ear, J.P. gave her another hug and walked outside. He thanked God for Grams. She was an amazing woman with a heart as big as all outdoors. That little slip of a woman with graying hair held a piece of his heart.

"J.P., what are you grinning about, boy?" Tate yelled from the basketball court.

"About how bad Marcus and I are going to wipe the court with you and Kevin."

"Oh, it's like that, white boy? You've been away pushing papers for a while. I see it's time for a reality check."

Marcus joined in, saying, "We're burning daylight. Best two out of three. Let's go." With that they began an aggressive game that lasted for the next hour and a half, ending with J.P. and Marcus winning by two points. Laughing and ragging on each other, they walked in the kitchen door. J.P. stopped mid-step when he saw Sidney sitting at the kitchen table.

Chapter Seven

Rushing past J.P., Sidney's brothers greeted her, giving her hugs and kisses, asking when she got in, how long she'd be home, just loving on her. J.P. stood frozen, staring, trying to get his mind to register that it was Sidney. So many thoughts were going through his mind, a part of him wanted to go to her, to hold her, to touch her, just to make sure she was real. Another part wanted to demand where she had been, and why she had left him. He was so not prepared for this moment, and was having a hard time sorting out all the emotions hitting him all at once: love, anger, longing and fear. *Easy, Carter,* he cautioned himself; all this time he had prayed for the chance to talk with her to understand what happened between them. Taking a deep breath, he calmed himself. He had waited what seem like a lifetime for this moment, and didn't want to blow it now. Pushing all his emotions aside, and taking on a casual appearance that he did not feel, he smiled and said, "Hello, Sidney, how are you? It's good to see you." J.P. walked over and gave her a brief hug. When he put his arms around her, a jolt of electricity went through his body so strongly that he couldn't form words. Clearing his throat, he realized she had said something to him. "I'm sorry; I didn't hear you."

"Hi, it's good to see you, too. How was the game?"

"Good, we won. How was the drive?"

"Long. Traffic was kind of bad so it took longer than planned."

J.P. couldn't stand it any longer, making small talk with her, when all he wanted was to hold her again and find out what happened. "I have to go; it's good seeing you again." With that he walked over to Grams and said, "I got to go." He kissed her on the cheek and headed for the door with Marcus following right behind him.

When they got to J.P.'s truck, Marcus asked in a voice filled with concern, "Dude, you okay?"

"No, I am a lot of things right now, but okay is not one of them. Where did she come from? What is she doing here?" Not waiting for an answer, he went on, "I need to clear my head. I'll call you later."

"Promise?" Marcus asked.

"Promise."

≈≈≈

Sidney told herself that she could do it; she could face J.P. and be okay. After all, the man was married and probably had a couple of kids. She had also hoped that he had also gained thirty pounds and was losing his hair. Well, that hadn't happened—the man was gorgeous, and he had gained weight in all the right places. *Yeah I think they call it muscle.* His dark-brown hair was a little wet from sweating. He looked so good; she could only stare. When he gave her a polite hug, her mind went south; she said something, but for the life of her, she didn't know if it made sense. No wonder he asked her again what she had said. The man must have thought she was some deranged woman, with lots of issues. Any sane man would have left to go home to his beautiful wife and children instead of hanging around having a crazy woman gawking at him. *See, Lord, I can't do this. Please take these feelings away, I don't want to love him, but after seeing him tonight I know I still do.*

≈≈≈

Marcus watched J.P. drive away, saying a prayer for him. Turning, he marched into the house, heading straight for Sidney. He knew Sidney; they were very close. She would tell him anything and still did, except when it came to J.P. That subject she refused to discuss with Marcus, but he knew she loved J.P., and he knew that he and J.P. weren't the only ones hurting when she left. When Sidney first went away to college, he could feel her hurt and hear it in their conversations. She tried to hide it, but he knew. Being twins gave them a close bond; they could feel each other's pain and sometimes think each other's thoughts. Yet when it came to J.P., she was a closed book, and over the years she built a wall that not even Marcus could get beyond. He didn't know what happened between Sidney and J.P. and nearly came to blows with J.P., thinking he had done something to Sidney to make her leave home. But, after a heated conversation and seeing just how much J.P. was hurt by her leaving, Marcus apologized for thinking the worst of his friend. Regardless of the wall Sidney built, Marcus was amazed at how tuned-in she was to J.P. Long after she left and all through college, she would call and tell him to check on J.P. or to give him a call. She always knew when J.P. was hurting, and every time she was spot-on about it. He wondered how she could be so connected to J.P. and yet refuse to talk to him or about him. Marcus didn't understand why she left and was hurt that she didn't tell him the reason, but he knew deep down that the connection she shared with J.P. was special.

Although they attended different colleges, Marcus and J.P. always stayed in touch and spent some weekends together. Since they grew up with each other, their friendship went beyond just being friends; they were more like brothers. Marcus knew that he could trust J.P. with anything and would tell him everything. There were no secrets between them, except when it came to Sidney. She made him promise not to mention she prompted him to check on J.P., and J.P. was no better, making Marcus promise not to mention that they had made Sidney a partner when they started the TCHD Crew Company. J.P. had reasoned that he and Sidney had created the project, and he wanted to see if it succeeded before sharing it with her when she returned. Marcus shook his head, frustrated with them both. He was convinced that Sidney loved J.P. then, and after seeing them together tonight, he was even more convinced of that. He saw the longing in her eyes and he saw the hurt; he just couldn't understand why, and it was high time he did.

As he headed into the house, so deep in thought about Sidney and J.P., Marcus didn't notice someone in his path until he collided with her. "Whoa!" he said, reaching out to steady the woman he'd bumped into. "I'm so sorry. Are you okay..." The words died on Marcus' lips as he encountered the bluest eyes he had ever seen. The word *wow* almost slipped out before he regained his voice and noticed he was still holding the woman's arms. He released her and asked again, "Are you okay? I'm sorry; I didn't see you."

"It's okay; I'm used to being bumped around catching the New York subway. Hi, I'm Stephanie."

"It's good to bump into you, Stephanie," he said with a smile. "What brings you to Resting Place?"

"I'm a friend of Sidney's."

"Aw Sidney, my twin; I'm looking for her." Just then Sidney walked up, and Marcus reached for her hand and said, "Hey, sis, you and me. We need to talk, now."

"Okay, Marcus, but I can't right now. Can we do it after Grams goes to bed?"

Marcus looked into her eyes with a slow smile. Sidney recognized that look, which meant whatever he needed to talk about was really important, and said, "Okay, my room after Grams goes to bed." Smiling, he turned to Stephanie.

"It was nice bumping into you, Stephanie. See you around."

Stephanie gave a shy reply, "See you around," and then watched him walk away.

"Okay, what was that about with Marcus?" Sidney asked with a raised eyebrow while sitting on Stephanie's bed a few minutes later.

"Nothing. He wasn't looking where he was going, and he just ran into me."

"Well, since you two have met, what do you think about Marcus?"

"He's nice and no; I'm not interested." Stephanie said, not sure what she was feeling. She wanted to get alone and think about her first meeting with Sidney's brother, Marcus. With other guys, she had never experienced the reaction she had with Marcus. If she could give it a name, it would be attraction, and when he flashed a smile her way, her pulse began to dance. Yes, she had to process this, and soon. Changing the subject, Stephanie asked, "What's up with the 'you and me now' command?"

"He'll want to know what's going on with J.P. Stephanie, I saw him, and girl, I was dumbstruck. I couldn't help it. He'll probably give me a lecture about J.P. being married and to get a grip. I'll talk with him later."

"Are you okay, Sidney? I mean with J.P.?"

"Steph, it was one of the hardest things I have ever had to do. Making small talk with him and acting like there was nothing between us. I know it's just one-sided, but it still hurts."

"I'm sorry, Sidney. I'll wait up for you in case you need to talk. I want to check my e-mail to see if anything has come back on the proposals for Phoenix we submitted to those three companies."

"Steph, you've been working non-stop ever since you became a partner of Phoenix. I know we're working with a short timeframe; seriously, Steph, it's our first night and a Friday, and it's a beautiful, summer night! Relax, go downstairs and visit with Marcus. . ."

"Sidney, I told you. . ."

"Yeah, I heard you, but a girl can hope," Sidney said, grinning as she left Stephanie's room.

≈≈≈

Sidney's back home…

J.P. struggled with what just happened; one minute he was playing ball with the guys, the next minute he was making small talk with Sidney Weston.

There she was…

He couldn't have dreamed up a more beautiful picture. She looked amazing, still slender and still curvy. She was beautiful at seventeen; now as a woman, she was breathtaking. The coal-black hair Sidney inherited from her Cherokee great-grandmother was longer and looked so confined in the ponytail she wore. Her smooth, brown skin was perfect, and when he hugged her for just a moment, it was like she was the missing piece to his soul, and she just fit. Nothing ever felt so good or so right. Out of all the women J.P. had known, and thanks to his father, dated, none of them had generated the response that Sidney produced within seconds of seeing her and in one brief hug. How was he supposed to deal with her now? If they had been meeting for the first time he would pursue her without question, but not knowing what happened between them caused fear of more rejection to grip his heart.

J.P. pondered a casual friendship with Sidney and grimaced in disgust at the thought. He certainly couldn't treat her as a casual friend. He'd known her most of his life. They had always been close, from the first day they had met on the basketball court. Their relationship had never been casual, and it didn't feel casual tonight when he hugged her. That hug generated sparks everywhere, and he wondered if she felt them, too.

The ringing phone halted his racing thoughts. "Hello?"

"J.P.?"

"Hi, Marcus."

"How are you doing? Are you okay?"

"Yeah, I'm okay; I was just caught off guard tonight."

"Grams had told me that Sidney was thinking about coming home. I would have told you, but every time I mention Sidney, you tell me you don't want to talk about her. I'm sorry; maybe I should have tried harder."

"It's okay, Marcus. Maybe seeing her and talking about what happened will give me some closure so I can move on."

"J.P. you're still in love with her." It wasn't a question.

"Marcus, I don't want to be, but I am, and I don't know what to do about it."

"I think she still cares, too, J.P. I think you guys really need to sit down and talk."

"I agree; we do need to talk." J.P. tried not to sound interested but asked, "Is she dating anyone?"

Marcus, missing nothing, asked, "Are you thinking about asking her for a date?" Without waiting for an answer he continued, "That's a great idea, why don't you give her a call and asked her out? Then you guys can talk."

The fear of rejection grew in J.P.'s heart at that moment and he said, 'I don't know, Marcus, maybe we should just leave it alone. It has been ten years."

Ignoring his statement, Marcus asked, "Do you love my sister? Because if you do, she is worth praying about and asking God what to do."

Pushing past the fear, J.P. said, "Okay, I'll pray about it."

With a smile in his voice, Marcus said, "Great. In the meantime, I'll be praying God's will for both of you."

"Thanks, Marcus, that means a lot, but on another less complicated subject, did your assistant get a chance to schedule Ms. Stephanie Reed from Phoenix for an appointment?"

Switching to business Marcus answered, "Yes, she did, but Wednesday wasn't good for Ms. Reed. It seems they are working with a short deadline and need to meet before next Wednesday. The only other day the members are available is tomorrow, Saturday, at 9:00 a.m. Will that work for you?"

J.P. replied, "Yeah, that sounds good to me. I would like to meet Ms. Reed and see if we can move forward with this proposal."

As he hung up the phone, J.P. looked up and said, "Lord, I don't know what has brought Sidney home, but I need your help. I don't know what to do here." After he prayed, a Scripture came to mind. *Trust in the Lord with all your heart and lean not on your own understanding; in all your ways acknowledge Him, and He shall direct your path.*

"Okay, Lord."

Chapter Eight

Sidney knocked on Marcus' bedroom door before entering, "Hi."

"Hey, Ney, it's been a while. I've missed you." Marcus said, using his nickname for Sidney. He opened his arms, and she walked into them and held him tight.

"I've missed you, too, Marc. It feels so good to be home. I didn't realize how much I've missed everybody."

"Ney, are you going to tell me why you left and didn't come back?" he asked.

Sidney looked into his eyes and saw the pain that her separation had caused him. He didn't have to say anything else; she could feel the hurt. She wrapped her arms around him again and said, "Marc, I'm so sorry." They were so close growing up; they shared everything. Being in his room, talking with him, connecting with him, made her long to tell him what happened. How many times had she picked up the phone to call him and pour her heart out to him? He would have listened to all her fears, all her hopes, but she couldn't risk Grams losing her house. Sidney also knew that after seeing J.P. tonight and realizing the depth of her feelings, she needed time to sort through her emotions. She couldn't say anything now. She had already made up her mind that she would tell Marcus and J.P. why she left. She had carried this burden alone long enough. After she talked with Grams about her financial situation, she would tell them everything.

Marcus pulled back and looked into her eyes and said, "Tell me, Sidney, why did you leave?"

"I want to tell you, and I will, but I can't right now. I need to talk with Grams about her finances first." Sidney knew that would buy her a little time.

Then Marcus caught her off guard by asking, "You still love J.P., don't you?" Before she could respond, they heard a scream and a crash from the kitchen.

They both bolted for the door to see what happened and found Grams at the foot of the stairs grabbing her arm in pain. Marcus' years of training while volunteering for the local rescue squad kicked in as he assessed the situation and took charge. "Sidney, get Tate and then call 911!" Sidney nodded and ran, calling for Tate, who came up from the basement with Kevin at his heels.

"What happened?" Tate asked as he evaluated his grandmother, his military experience as a medic serving him well. He bent over Grams, determined that her right arm was broken and checked to see if she had any other injuries. Sidney met Stephanie in the hallway, and told her about Grams' fall. Together they rushed to the phone to call 911. Tate yelled into the kitchen, "Sidney tell them we're on our way to the hospital." He picked up his grandmother and held her in his arms as he headed to Kevin's truck.

Sidney yelled back, "We're right behind you. Be careful!"

≈≈≈

Still half asleep, J.P. groped for his cell phone. "Hello."

"J.P., its Marcus. I'm at the hospital with Grams; she's had a fall."

"What? Is she okay? What happened?"

"She fell down the hall stairs. She had left her medication in the kitchen and didn't have any shoes on and slipped on the steps."

"I'll be right there." J.P. was up and moving.

"No, J.P. You need to meet with Ms. Reed at 9:00 a.m. tomorrow... or today." Marcus suddenly realized it was past midnight. "They just took her down for x-rays. I think we'll be here for a few more hours, so I won't be at the meeting."

"Don't worry; I'll take care of the meeting. I'll stop by later to see her. Call me if anything changes with Grams, and I'll let you know how the meeting turns out." Hanging up, J.P. said a prayer of thanksgiving to God for sparing Grams from a more serious injury. He didn't understand how God answered some prayers while others went unanswered. He had prayed and believed God for his relationship with Sidney. He had trusted God to bring her back to him and had waited, but God didn't answer. After hearing nothing from her for a few years, J.P. stopped asking, thinking that it didn't make sense to keep hoping for something that wasn't going to happen. Then the thought came to him. *She did come back. She's back now.*

Shaking his head, J.P. got out of bed and headed for the shower, realizing that it was no use trying to get back to sleep. He reasoned that if he got an early start at work, maybe it would take his mind off Sidney. After just a few minutes in her presence, his head was full of thoughts about her, and his heart ached for something that no longer existed, a future with Sidney.

Chapter Nine

Stephanie entered the TCHD Crew building, a little surprised that a company of this magnitude would be located in the small town of Resting Place. She had researched several companies large enough to support the Burke contract. TCHD, although relatively young, less than five years in business, had acquired a number of huge contracts, including one with the federal government, making it the best choice. She and Sidney had prayed about the risks involved in going into business with this young company, and decided that if God opened the door for them, they would walk through it. So, this meeting today would determine if they could move forward with a partnership. Since Laura Burke had given Phoenix only thirty days to partner with a larger company, the timing of this meeting was crucial.

Sidney had planned to be with Stephanie today, she and Marcus waited with Grams to talk with her doctor, and there was no way to know how long it would take. Stephanie asked if she should reschedule the meeting, but Sidney said, "No, we don't have the time to reschedule. You go to the meeting, and if you like them, accept the partnership. I trust your judgment."

"Are you sure, Sid?"

"Yes, Partner, I'm sure. Let's get together after the meeting, so you can fill me in."

≈≈≈

At 8:55 a.m., Stephanie walked alone into the executive office suite. "Good morning," a woman greeted her from behind the reception desk.

"Good morning, I'm Stephanie Reed; I have a nine o'clock appointment."

The woman stood, extended, her hand and said, "Hi, Ms. Reed, it's good to meet you. I'm Maggie Hart. Would you like some coffee? Since its Saturday, our admin staff is off, but I can make a pot."

"No, thank you; I'm okay." Ms. Hart's warm greeting set Stephanie at ease. She had a knack for reading people, a gift she used often at Bolen IT. Looking at Ms. Hart, she noticed her striking red hair; it was long and straight reaching below her waistline. She appeared to be in her mid to late twenties. She was a beautiful woman. Stephanie could tell that she had a kindness that drew people. She felt comfortable with Ms. Hart, and that gave her a little more confidence that the meeting would go well.

A tall, handsome man in a dark-blue business suit walked into the office, balancing a carton of coffee and a box of donuts. "Good morning. Let me take these into the conference room. Maggie, can you get some plates and cups?"

"Sure. Stephanie, we'll be right back." Stephanie's nervousness flared up again. She had to remind herself that she had made numerous presentations for projects, and this shouldn't be any different—but it *was* different! Sidney had asked her to be a partner in the Phoenix Company. Sidney believed in *her,* and she couldn't let her down! Closing her eyes, Stephanie sent up a silent prayer. *Oh Lord, please give me wisdom concerning this merger.*

After the arrival of the food, the other board members came in right at nine, offered greetings and headed into the board room. As Stephanie waited, the man with the donuts and coffee walked toward her, extending his hand. "Hi, I'm John Carter, Ms. Reed. It's good to meet you. Would you like to join us? We're ready to begin the meeting." He escorted her to a large conference room with four people sitting at the table.

Once seated, Mr. Carter said, "Ms. Reed, thank you for taking the time to meet with us today. We're not very formal around here, so please call me John. A couple of our board members were not able to attend the meeting today, but they have shared their input concerning your proposal. Allow us to introduce ourselves to you." The board members introduced themselves and talked a little about their position in the company.

As they went around, Stephanie began to relax, and her excitement grew. By the time they were finished, she was ready to share about Phoenix and their hopes for a partnership. An hour and a half later the meeting was still going with high energy, and Stephanie fit right in with the group.

Everyone was engaged; the board members were asking her questions and about her ideas, sharing their experiences with past projects. There was a natural synergy in the room. Stephanie was surprised when John said, "I hate to end the meeting, but we only scheduled it for one hour. Having already exceeded that time, we still need to discuss a couple more items in the contract."

Blushing with embarrassment, Stephanie began to apologize, but John raised his hand and said, "No need. I think I can speak for the board when I say we have enjoyed this time and discussion. Any other day, time would not be a factor, but since this is the weekend, some of us have family commitments. So at this time, we want to address your conditions for the partnership," J.P. stated, looking at the proposal packet. "The board agrees with the condition to establish satellite offices, and the stipulation that current employees retain their jobs and salaries. The third condition for board membership is an issue for us. Our board is made up of the founding members and their families; we do not open it for membership. With that being said, I see that this is an important issue for you. Can you share with us why membership to the board means so much? We have merged with a few other companies, and board membership has never been requested."

Stephanie considered his words before speaking, "My partner and I are concerned that our vision and core values remain long after we merge with a company. We would also like input into any major changes that would affect Phoenix."

Thoughtfully considering her words, John spoke again, "Our vision and values are very similar and each board member holds to them. Would you be willing to discuss our position with your partner and consider modifying the contract to address your concerns? We will favorably consider any reasonable modification."

Stephanie smiled and agreed with his suggestions. As she left the conference room, she was excited about the possibilities and the successful meeting. *Thank you, God!*

≈≈≈

Heading home, Stephanie thought about the changes in her life since meeting Sidney Weston. Stephanie tended not to trust anyone, experiencing at a young age that trusting only led to disappointment. Her dad demonstrated that when he walked out on his family after her mom became too sick to care for herself. He couldn't handle it and left. Then her school friends began to fade away. They couldn't handle it. Everyone left, even her best friend, Jane Farrow. Stephanie and Jane had been friends since the first grade, but Jane couldn't handle it. One day Stephanie looked around, and no one was there for her and her mom. Everyone had left. That day she was forced to face the hard fact that she couldn't depend on anyone. Meeting Sidney changed all that.

Stephanie had never known anyone like Sidney, who loved in the hard times. Stephanie was at her lowest point when they met. Instead of firing her for coming in late almost every day and taking long breaks to check on her mom, Sidney jumped right in and started helping, first by leading her to Christ. Stephanie held that day as the greatest day of her life. Sidney never left, even when Stephanie's mom became really ill at the end. Sidney cried with her, and she *did not leave.* Stephanie began to tear up just thinking about how much God must love her to put Sidney in her life. Tucking those thoughts away for later, she pulled into Grams' driveway. Stephanie hopped out of the car, heading for Sidney to fill her in on the meeting.

"How's Grams?" Stephanie asked as she walked in the kitchen, putting her briefcase on a chair at the table and dropping into the chair beside Sidney.

"She's good, embarrassed about the fall. She has a broken arm, so she has a cast and will have to take it easy for a while. She can come home tomorrow." Sidney paused and said, "Steph, it could have been so much worse; we're grateful that she's okay."

"Me, too."

"How did the meeting go with TCHD? Are they interested in our proposal?"

"Yes, they are! Our meeting was scheduled for an hour, but we went on for almost two hours! I think they like what we can bring to their company, and the fact that we have the Burke Company didn't hurt."

It's really great of Laura to give us this chance before requesting other bids."

"Sidney, Laura believes in you. Ever since you started the Phoenix Company and created jobs for the church members, she has supported you. You know Laura was really upset with how you were treated by Mr. Feeling. She gave me a call before she left for England and asked for the company names of some of your other clients. She said she wanted some references from them."

Sidney replied, "I guess it's their process when signing a contract. Laura is a blessing, and I don't want to let her down. So tell me about this two-hour meeting."

Stephanie gave her a brilliant smile and began telling her about how nice the people were and how it felt as if she had known them forever. Then she told Sidney that they agreed with two of their conditions, but not the third one.

Sidney said, "The membership one, right?"

"Yeah, only the founding members and their family members can hold membership. However, they did ask if we would consider modifying the contract to address our concerns. "

"I can't blame them. I would have done the same thing. Okay, let's see if we can come up with language that will protect us and secure this partnership."

Chapter Ten

Sidney sat quietly in the hospital room and watched her grandmother sleeping peacefully. Grams awakened briefly when the nurse brought her pain medication at midnight, and then drifted back to sleep, unaware that Sidney was sitting there. Sidney used this quiet time to talk with God about why she was home. She thought about how many people who she loved had suffered because of her leaving: Marcus, Grams, Kevin and Tate, her friends from school, friends from church and, of course, J.P. She hated the secret that had caused her to leave everything and everyone she loved. Seeing J.P. again was almost more than she could stand. Sidney knew her feelings ran deep for him, but after the other night…. Ten years melted away in minutes, being in his presence. She still hadn't figured out how she would survive the pain of seeing him happy with his family.

Sidney had lost so much because of Mr. Carter, but no more. She resolved in her heart that he would not take another thing from her. She would tell her family the truth and would rebuild her life and relationships here in Resting Place. Once she had made that decision, peace settled in her heart, and she knew that God had led her home to stay. She went over to her grandmother and kissed her forehead and said, "I love you Grams. See you tomorrow." As she turned to leave, Sidney walked right into J.P.

≈≈≈

J.P. waited all day to visit Grams, even though he wanted to go see her when Marcus called last night. Grams was hurt, and he wanted to be with her. J.P. loved Grams; she was like a mother to him and he needed to see for himself that she was alright. He hated the feeling of helplessness he'd felt when he was eight, watching his mom fade away. Marcus said Grams was okay, but he needed to find out for himself. Another reason J.P. waited was because he didn't want to run into Sidney again until he could sort out what he would say to her. After talking with Marcus, he couldn't stop thinking about her and wondered if he could pursue her. In his heart of hearts, he knew if there were the slightest possibility, he would, but fear continued to plague him. He needed to know if Sidney left because of him.

As J.P. walked into Grams' room, he ran into someone and reached out to steady her. His eyes met Sidney's and time stood still and for the briefest of moments. He saw longing and something else, but before he could understand the look, she pulled away as if his touch burned her. A little breathless, she asked, "J.P. what are you doing here?"

"I came to see Grams. I just wanted to make sure she was alright." Looking over at Grams, he asked, "How is she?"

"She's better; they're going to release her tomorrow."

As Sidney spoke, J.P. stared at her, wondering if this was the time to talk about the past. He had to know. "Sidney what happened?"

Sidney just stared at him; knowing exactly what J.P. was talking about. His gentle words caught her off guard. She had expected indifference, anger, even sarcasm, but she didn't expect to see hurt and hope. Looking into his liquid brown eyes and seeing him like this was more than she could stand. She turned away.

J.P. was encouraged. That look Sidney gave him before she turned away caused his heart to beat triple-time, and he was drawn to her. He moved closer to her and put his hands on her shoulders, and slowly turned her around to face him and asked ever so gently, "Sidney, did I do something wrong? Did I hurt you?"

She started to look away again, but he reached out and cupped her chin, gently but firmly enough that she couldn't look away.

J.P. looked into her eyes, those beautiful brown eyes, and he could see what she did not say. He saw love and longing and despair. "Sidney?"

Sidney couldn't stand it anymore, she wanted to tell J.P. everything, but it wasn't the time. She had to talk with Grams first and find out about the house. However, she would not let J.P. think that it was his fault that she left. She would give him that. "No, it wasn't you; you didn't do anything wrong."

J.P. held her gaze then his eyes dropped to her lips. They were parted as if she was going to say more. He moved closer; he couldn't help it. This was Sidney, and for the first time in years his heart was beating almost out of his chest. He brushed his lips over hers, and she kissed him back. J.P. felt his broken heart begin to heal, and then overflow with love for her. He realized that he wanted her and no one else, and if he had to win her love again he would. He deepened the kiss, reveling in how good Sidney felt in his arms, how right it felt to hold her.

Then J.P. felt Sidney stiffen in his arms. When he pulled back to look at her, she had a strange look on her face, a look of guilt. "Sidney—I..." Before he could say more, she ran out of the room as if her life depended on getting away from him, leaving J.P. bewildered as to what had just happened.

≈≈≈

J.P. stayed with Grams, seated beside her bed, watching her sleep peacefully and reliving that awesome kiss with Sidney. He realized two things; one, he was even more confused about why Sidney left, and two, she still had feelings for him! Remembering her e-mail, hope flared up in him again. *Father, please guide me. I still love her. Can it be that she still loves me? Help me to know what to do Lord; I can't lose her again.*

In the early hours of the morning, Grams woke up to find J.P. still sitting by her bed, asleep. "J.P.? Baby, what are you doing here?"

Seeing that she was awake, J.P. got up, went to her bedside and kissed her cheek. "Hi, Grams, how do you feel?"

"I'm fine, just a broken bone; it will heal. How are you?"

"I'm good, Grams." J.P. said trying not to look into her all-seeing, hazel eyes.

"Now, J.P., if I felt better, I would box your ears for lying." Grams said with a smile.

"Grams, you knew how I felt about Sidney; I thought we had something special, but she left without a word."

"Baby, I knew you loved that girl, and I knew Sidney loved you. I waited for you to come and tell me how you felt. I would have told you where she was."

"Grams, I don't think she wanted me to find her. Do you know why she left?"

"No. The night after the prom she told me that she thought it would be better for everybody if she went to college in New York. I knew she didn't want to go to New York. Sidney never even mentioned going away to college, but she had this determined look in her eyes; I knew I couldn't talk her out of it, and sure enough, she left right after graduation. She's never told me why."

"Grams, I think it's time we found out why. I want to see her again, Grams, but I don't want the past to get in the way. It's just so hard when I don't know what happened."

"J.P., God will work this out. Trust Him to show you what you need to do for Sidney."

≈≈≈

Sidney sat in her room warring between bliss and shame. J.P.'s kiss was everything it used to be and more, everything she had dreamed about; it felt so good in his arms. But J.P. was a married man, and how could she throw herself at a married man? *Lord please forgive me. I can't do this; I can't be around him, but I can't leave Resting Place again either. Oh Lord, what do I do now?"*

A soft knock sounded at her door, followed by Stephanie's concerned voice, "Sidney, can I come in?"

"Yes."

Stephanie took one look at her, then rushed over to her and hugged her tightly. Sidney broke down and cried as her heart broke all over again. After the tears subsided, Stephanie asked, "What happened? You haven't cried like that since you found out J.P. was engaged. Oh—you saw J.P.?"

"I saw him, Steph. I thought he would be indifferent like he was the other night or even mad at me, but Steph, he was hurt, and he asked me if he had done something wrong to make me leave. When I told him no, he kissed me—and I kissed him back."

"What happened? What did you do?"

"I ran. Steph, I don't know what to do! I want to run away, but I know I can't leave, and he's married. I should never have kissed him back, but I couldn't help myself. Steph I just need to stay away from him."

"Sidney, are you sure he's married? Because if he is, what is he doing kissing on you?"

"Stephanie, you remember J.P.'s dad sent me a wedding invitation a few months after I heard that he was engaged."

"Sidney, something is not right here. Either he is a sleaze bag for cheating on his wife, or he's not married. Something's not right."

"Stephanie, I don't know what's going on, but I do know I need to stay away from that man."

≈≈≈

Sunday morning Sidney attended church with Marcus. Stephanie had volunteered to stay with Grams since she was still on some rather strong pain medication. After making up her mind to stay away from J.P., Sidney started her own personal pity party, looking at everything that had been taken from her and feeling that somehow she deserved the way things had worked out. She was getting restless and thinking about leaving again; she needed answers. Today she needed to hear from God.

As Sidney entered the church where she had grown up, she felt the presence of God and began to relax.   She saw Pastor Michael Greene, affectionately called Pastor Mike, talking with Susie, the church secretary, before the service started.   Pastor Mike came to Resting Place as a young pastor, fresh out of seminary. Many people felt he wouldn't stay long, but as time passed they realized Pastor Mike loved the work God had called him to do, and he loved the people with whom God entrusted him.

One of Pastor Mike's early sermons was entitled, "With Cords of Love." Sidney remembered that he said he would follow the Lord's example, and he would draw the people with cords of love. God has blessed him to do just that. The church and the local community loved and respected Pastor Mike.

Sidney made a mental note to talk with Pastor Mike about Phoenix and the employment opportunities that would be extended to the congregation. Hearing the opening hymn, she took her seat next to Marcus. She had really missed her home church, and realized that she really needed to be there today. As the last song finished, out of the corner of her eye she saw J.P. enter and take a seat in the back row.

Determined to stay focused, Sidney fixed her eyes on Pastor Mike as he began to speak in a strong, baritone voice, *"But God has chosen the foolish things of the world to put to shame the wise, and God has chosen the weak things of the world to put to shame the things which are mighty. 1 Corinthians 1: 27."* Sidney listened as he talked about how God uses the foolish things to confound the wise and the unlikely, or the weaker things to shame the strong. Pastor Mike went on the say that God chooses His people; He places them in positions and allows them to be promoted or achieve positions that others may not feel that they should have or to deserve. She wanted to say "Amen" to that.

Pastor Mike looked around the church and asked, "Have you ever thought that God allowed you to get to the place you are because He wants to use you for His purpose, for His glory? You may be the messenger of God's grace or God's judgment."

About half-way through the sermon, Sidney realized that God was talking directly to her. He had purposed her to be at Bolen IT, and she had been there for His glory. She realized that she was good enough for the position, not because of her hard work or her great skill, but because God wanted her there for His purpose. Sidney was humbled at the thought that God would use her to bring glory to His name. By the time the sermon was over, Sidney's pity party was long gone and replaced with joy that God's will was done at Bolen IT. She was the unlikely, the least expected, the unwanted, but God used her to challenge them and maybe change them. Wow, God, what are You up to with Bolen IT?

After service was over, Sidney volunteered to take Mrs. Wilson, one of the Church Mothers, home, effectively avoiding any encounter with J.P. Carter. Leaving the building, she chatted with Mrs. Wilson about how much she enjoyed the service—doing everything she could to keep her thoughts from drifting back to J.P.

≈≈≈

A few days later, J.P. was deep in thought when Marcus walked in his office with the Phoenix proposal. "Hey, you look a million miles away."

"I was thinking about Sidney; I saw her last week."

"Did you get to talk with her?"

J.P. blushed, thinking of the kiss he shared with Sidney, and said, "We talked a little, but it was more what I saw in her eyes. Marcus, I think she still cares for me, which make this whole thing even more confusing."

"Sidney has never been able to hide her feelings. I know she still cares."

"Then what made her leave?"

"I asked her the night Grams fell."

"What did she say?"

"She said she wanted to tell me, but she had to talk with Grams about her finances first."

"Is Grams okay financially, Marcus? Cause if she needs anything, let me know."

"Grams is fine; that's one thing Sidney made sure of. She went to school full-time and worked a full-time job and sent almost all her paycheck home with a note for Grams to put it toward the mortgage." After a while, the rest of us guys starting sending money home as well. Grams' finances are great.

"Grams had a loan with our bank, didn't she?"

"She still does. She had some renovations done last fall and refinanced the mortgage to pay for it."

"Maybe I need to look at her account history and see what was going on back then."

Marcus closed J.P.'s office door. "Let's pray and ask God to show us what caused Sidney to leave, and that His will be done concerning you and Sidney."

As they joined hands, J.P. looked Marcus in the eyes and said, "I still love her, Marcus."

"I believe she loves you too, J.P." Then Marcus prayed for guidance and God's help to reveal every hidden deed.

Chapter Eleven

Roy Feeling entered the conference room with a folder in his hand. Once seated at the table, he looked around at his senior executive team, took a deep breath and began talking. "We have a problem. The Burke Company has decided not to sign on with us." Taking a folded sheet of paper out of the folder, he said, "We received this letter from Mrs. Laura Burke, Vice President." He began to read the letter.

Dear Mr. Feeling,

The purpose of the letter is to inform you that after careful consideration, we have decided to retract our offer to work with your company.

Prior to our decision to sign with Bolen IT, we met with Ms. Sidney Weston on several occasions. We are meticulous in our business practices and wanted to be sure that Bolen IT could and would represent us in a manner consistent with our values. We were confident that Ms. Weston would be able to do just that.

Sidney Weston was an excellent representative for Bolen IT, and her work ethic and professionalism made our upcoming transition appear seamless, so much so, that after speaking and meeting with her, we were not only impressed with the caliber of Bolen's employees, but also the organization as a whole. Needless to say we were very surprised and disappointed to hear of Ms. Weston's recent departure from your organization.

In the three weeks since Ms. Weston's departure, we have had numerous concerns with Bolan IT's communications and customer service. These concerns have prompted me to contact some of my colleagues who also received services from Ms. Weston. My communication with them confirmed that they have had similar concerns. I cannot speak for my colleagues, but we are very disappointed in the standard of service your company is currently providing and fear that this standard will continue.

Therefore, we feel that it is in the best interest of the Burke Company to retract our letter of intent to sign with Bolen IT. We have made arrangements with another company that we feel is more suitable for the high standard of service we require.

Respectfully,
Laura Burke, Vice President
Burke Company

After reading the letter he looked around the room again, then took another deep breath and asked with a clipped voice, "Do you realize what she just said? She said, in other words, Bolen IT is substandard, that we are not good enough to manage their account. I was also informed by one of our contacts at the Burke Company that the only reason they wanted to sign with us was because Sidney Weston would be handling their account."

Mr. Feeling opened the folder, shuffled some papers and spoke again, "The Dalton Agency has contacted us and informed us that they will not be renewing their contract at the end of this month. This is also one of Sidney's accounts. Dalton has been with us for four years now. One of our newest clients, Perkins Electronics, has also stated that they would like to cancel their account with us. Their contract identified Sidney Weston as their contract representative, and since she is no longer with Bolen IT, they have decided to cancel the contract. Folks, we have a problem. These are three of the largest accounts we have; losing them will be a major financial loss to this company."

One of the board members asked, "If it's Sidney they want, can we get her back?"

Roy dropped his head and said, "No, we can't get her back; that is a bridge that we have burned. She knows exactly why she didn't get that promotion, and she made it plain that she won't come back." Roy remembered the cold chill that came over him the day Sidney walked out of his office. He knew it was a mistake, but refused to follow his gut. He felt that since he built his business from the ground up, he couldn't bring himself to allow someone like Sidney to be his equal. Now he was afraid that the business he built might be falling apart.

Taking a moment to look around the room, Roy continued, "I have reviewed Sidney's Client Portfolio. Over the five years she was with Bolen IT, she established fifteen of our major accounts with fairly large companies as well as several small business accounts that are all currently active today. In comparison, over the last five years our other four junior executives collectively established twenty-five accounts and out of those, only twelve are major accounts. According to this data, Sidney Weston was a greater asset to this company than we knew." Roy Feeling rubbed his forehead, trying to ease the tension there before continuing. "In light of this development, I am calling an emergency meeting to discuss how we will proceed. If Sidney's other clients follow suit, we will be out of business in a matter of months. So until we find a way to retain her current contracts and acquire some new major contracts, we will remain in a crisis status. As of right now, all leave and vacation requests are disapproved and all bonuses and promotion requests, including the promotion to this executive board, are canceled until further notice. I suggest you go tell your people what's coming down the pike. Meeting adjourned."

≈≈≈

Stephanie came running in the kitchen, beaming shouting, "We got it! We got the partnership! We got the partnership! They accepted our terms. We're scheduled to sign the contract on Monday!"

Sidney gave her a big hug and said, "Steph, you rock! Congratulations, you did a great job, partner!"

Just then Stephanie's cell phone beeped indicating a text message. She read the text, frowned and said, "It's a text from Judy, from the contracting office at Bolen." Then she read it aloud.

Hi Stephanie, I'm texting because I can't risk calling on the phone. Tell Sidney to check her e-mail. A number of her old clients are looking for her. I have given them her e-mail address; I hope she doesn't mind. Things are getting really bad here. Several of Sidney's old clients are leaving Bolen and it's causing a stir. Let me know if a contracting position comes available. I am willing to relocate.

Sidney went to her room and pulled out her laptop while Stephanie texted Judy, "Stephanie! Stephanie! Come look at this!"

Stephanie ran up the stairs to Sidney's room and looked at her e-mails. "What?!"

"Six of my old clients want to know who I am working with because they want to work with me!"

"Oh no, that's what Judy was talking about."

"Steph, I think God is doing something at Bolen IT, and I am not getting in His way. God has shown me that I really was good enough for that promotion. I worked hard for Bolen IT, and I was qualified to be a senior executive there. I know now that God was using me for His purpose and for His glory. I thank God that He made me good enough to be there, not because of whom I know or the color of my skin. He gave me the ability to do it, and I know He will bless us at TCHD Crew Company. Steph, I finally got it, and I will never accept that lie again!" At that moment, Sidney felt a heaviness lift from her, and she realized how deeply ingrained the perception of not being good enough was in her heart. The freedom she received was evident in her countenance. Stephanie, seeing the change taking place, gave Sidney a hug. Seeing the peace and joy on Sidney's face, Stephanie said, "Welcome home, Sidney; welcome to your resting place."

Chapter Twelve

Stephanie sat on the back porch thinking about how God had moved in Sidney's and her lives. She marveled at how God worked it out for them to merge with TCHD Crew Company; how Sidney's old clients still wanted to work with them. She questioned God about J.P. being married; from what Sidney told her about him, he didn't act married. She sent up a prayer heavenward; *Father, give Sidney wisdom concerning J.P., and reveal to her if he is married or not.*

Then her thoughts shifted to Marcus; she had only known Sidney's twin for a few weeks, but every time she encountered him, her attraction for him grew. Marcus, like his sister was easy to talk with, and he possessed the same caring, gentle spirit Sidney had. They had talked a few times. Okay, every night since she arrived, while cleaning up the dishes after dinner. The dishes would be finished, but they would be in their own world, talking. Stephanie had never known anyone like Marcus, and she found herself hanging on his every word.

He shared stories about his school years with Sidney and J.P., and Stephanie could picture how close the three of them were. The more he talked about their relationship, the more she wanted to be a part of it. It dawned on her that she was thinking about a relationship with Marcus. Stephanie marveled at the attraction she felt for him; granted he was handsome, very handsome, and tall with pecan brown skin that was perfect. He had an athletic grace about him that caused people to take notice when he walked into a room. At least, it caused her to take notice. She liked him, a lot, but it wasn't just his good looks that drew her. It was he himself; there was a connection between them that defied logic and even common sense.

Marcus stirred emotions in Stephanie that she had never felt before, never dreamed of feeling, and he acted as if he cared about her, really cared about her. She overheard Marcus' brothers Kevin and Tate teasing him about wanting to do the dishes. Stephanie found herself hoping that he did care, and that they could be more than friends. Every time the word love came to her mind, she quickly pushed it away; however, it was getting harder and harder to push the word or her thoughts about Marcus Weston away.

≈≈≈

Marcus was turning off lights, heading to bed, when he saw Stephanie sitting on the back porch. His heart started beating double time. Lately, thoughts of Stephanie consumed his mind. Seeing her every day in passing and each time they talked while cleaning up the kitchen caused him to become even more fascinated with her. He had never been attracted to white women, but with Stephanie it didn't matter. Finally, he began to understand the relationship Sidney and J.P. had, where color didn't matter. He remembered asking Sidney why she liked J.P. so much, and was it because he was white. She told him that when she was with J.P., she never noticed that he was white, she just noticed him. He didn't understand her then, but now he realized that when he was with Stephanie, he didn't see her as white, he just saw her, and what he saw made him long for more.

Stephanie was special and beautiful and smart and kind and the list kept growing. Her blue eyes were amazing; Marcus found himself staring into them like a lovesick kid. He had given himself so many reasons why this relationship couldn't work and reminded himself so many times that he was never attracted to white women; then he would see her, or she would give him a shy smile, and all his good reasoning would disappear. He just liked her, and the more time he spent around her, the more he wanted to spend time around her. Smiling at that thought, he grabbed a couple of bottles of water and headed out the back door. "Hi, Stephanie."

She turned to see him and nervously push her hair behind her right ear, saying, "Hi, Marcus; I didn't know anyone else was still up."

"I was heading to bed when I saw the light. Would you like some company?"

She moved over to make room.

"Sure." He sat down beside her.

Stephanie wanted to know about something that puzzled her, "Can I ask you something?"

Marcus raised an eyebrow, "Sure."

"You and Sidney are twins, but you don't have twin names. Why?"

"Aw, but we do have twin names; mine is Marcus Nicolas Weston, and hers is Sidney Nicole Weston. Our mom used to tell us that first we are unique, and then we are twins."

"Wow, that's really cool; your mom sounds great."

"She was. She always made us feel that we could do anything. She and our dad were killed in a car accident when we were six years old. I really miss them." Realizing he had shared more than he intended, he changed the subject. "So what do you think about Resting Place?"

"It's great, not as fast paced as New York, but not too slow either, although that might change when we start working."

"There is a lot of history here."

"Really? I'd like to hear about it."

"Our mom used to tell us a story about Resting Place when we were really little. Kevin and Tate were older, so they may remember more than I do, but I always liked hearing it and telling it.

"Resting Place was founded by seven people and their families. In their childhood these seven all lived in the same town and went to school together and then went off to college together. Once they had gotten their degrees, they tried to get jobs in the town where they grew up, but no one would give them a chance. The town didn't want black doctors, Indian school teachers, Italian police, Jewish accountants, and Hispanic lawyers. The town's people claimed that there were no jobs in their field, but they wanted the seven to work blue-collar jobs, and they did for a time. Then one night they were holding a Bible study at the lawyer's house. After they finished the study, they joined hands and prayed. The Lord gave one of the members the Scripture, Matthew 11:28, which says, *Come to me all you who are weary and heavy laden, and I will give you rest.* Then one of the men in the group said, "I am tired, and I need His rest, but I know that I won't find it here. I think I'm going to start seeking until I find my resting place, where I can do what God has called me to do."

"That man continued to seek God for a place where he could move and be at rest. A few months later at the Bible study he shared with the group of a place he had found way out in Maryland that was for sale. It was nothing but woods, but he was convinced that God was calling him to go there. That night he asked the group to pray for him, that he would be able to raise the funds to buy some land. As they prayed, the Lord did an amazing thing, He touched everyone's heart with a desire to move to this place. So, over the next few months, they pooled their funds together and were able to buy seven acres of land. They cleared one plot and built one house. After that they all moved into that house and worked on another and another, until everybody had a home. Then they started building the town; a school, a store, a doctor's office, and other businesses."

"Whenever people asked them where they lived, they would say, 'Resting Place.' More people found out about the town and wanted to settle there too, some saying they were looking for rest. After the town had grown, they made it official and named it Resting Place, founded by Arthur Rose, our great, great, grandfather."

"Wow, there is a lot of history here. Thank you for sharing it. I can see how it got its name. It is very peaceful here, and it feels like a place where you can find yourself and be at rest."

"Do you think you might settle down here?"

"I'm not sure. Sidney and I haven't talked about it."

"You and Sidney are pretty close."

"Yes, we are. Sidney was my boss, but she was different; she cared about me. When she found out how sick my mom was, she latched on to me and wouldn't let go. I wasn't used to people caring about me or my mother, but Sidney did. She would visit my mom and pray with her, and she made sure we had what we needed. She never asked what we needed; she would watch and pray and then do it. When my mom got really sick and wanted to come home, Sidney said, 'Our mother wants to come home. Let's bring her home.'" Marcus listened with great pride for Sidney and growing affection for Stephanie.

Stephanie continued talking as if she needed to share this information. Marcus sat and listened, forming an understanding of the bond Sidney and

Stephanie shared. "The day my mother…" Stephanie's voice broke as tears streamed down her face. Marcus moved closer and put his arms around her. As he held her, a surge of protective feelings welled up inside him; he could see her pain, and the desire to comfort her and make things better was fierce.

Stephanie continued on, her voice so soft that Marcus had to strain to hear her. "The day my mom died, Sidney was with us. She told my mom that we were a family, and we would take care of each other and not to worry about us. My mom died in peace. Sidney was there for me and my mom. No one has ever cared about us like that, and because of that I would do anything for Sidney."

Silence fell except for Stephanie's sigh as she relaxed in Marcus' arms. His heart melted right then; he knew that Stephanie had changed his life. He asked himself how this could be. He didn't even know her last name, her favorite color or food. What he did know was that she was important to him, and for now, that was enough.

Stephanie pulled away, apologizing for being so emotional. Marcus lifted her chin and held her gaze, which stopped her from continuing. "Don't apologize." He wiped the lingering tears from her face with the pad of his thumb. Then he shared something that he had not voiced to anyone. "I was really angry with Sidney for a long time after she left. We were very close; she was my best friend, and we shared everything. It felt like I had lost a part of me. It hurt so badly, and I didn't know what to do with the pain, so I got mad. I was so angry with her for not sharing with me why she left or not trusting me enough to tell me what was going on. Now I can see that a part of her leaving involved meeting you and being there for you and your mom. It shows me that God had a purpose for her being in New York, and knowing that really helps."

Marcus continued to hold Stephanie as they grew quiet, comfortable, each in their own thoughts. Then she looked up, and the desire she saw in Marcus' eyes made her catch her breath. Marcus slowly lower his head and brushed his lips across hers. He pulled back slightly and waited giving her room to move away, but she didn't; he kissed her again, and her response was instant and sweet. CRASH! Startled, they broke apart and looked around to see a stray cat on the garbage can. Blushing, Stephanie said, "I'd better go in," and made a hasty retreat.

Marcus caught her hand and asked, "Are you okay? I'll apologize if you want me to, but I won't be sorry it happened."

Stephanie said in a soft voice, "I'm okay, and I'm not sorry either." Smiling she ran into the house.

Marcus stayed outside talking to the Lord about this amazing woman whom he knew so little about and yet she alone had accessed a part of his heart that until tonight had remained untouched. Marcus made a mental note to schedule lunch with J.P. to talk about Stephanie. He and J.P. had agreed in their early teens that before they did something stupid like fall in love, they would take a time out and talk about it. J.P. had that conversation when he was seventeen years old with Marcus about Sidney. Marcus had never wanted to talk with J.P. about anyone until now.

≈≈≈

Stephanie was up early the next morning, giving up on sleep. She kept reliving her time with Marcus the night before. So many emotions crowded her mind that she was up all night trying to make sense of it. Was it just a kiss? It didn't feel like just a kiss. She didn't have a lot of experience, but it felt special. Could she and Marcus have something special? He held her and kissed her as if she were precious to him, someone to be treasured. She had never experienced anything like it. She prayed and asked the Lord to lead her concerning him. *Lord, I could really fall hard for Marcus. Please show me Your will concerning him. I like so many things about him. Lord, don't let me fall for him if it isn't in Your will that we be together.*

"Good morning." Sidney said as she walked in the kitchen over to the coffee pot.

"Good morning."

Sidney stopped with the cup mid-air. "What's that look?"

"What look?"

"That look, you look different."

"What do you mean?"

Sidney put the cup down, walked to the table and said, "You are blushing. Have you been talking with Marcus?"

"Yeah, we've talked."

"When? You weren't blushing when I went to bed last night."

"Okay Sidney, we talked last night."

"And?"

"And what?"

"Do you like him?"

"Maybe."

"Okay, Stephanie, something's up, so tell me."

"Oh Sidney, I'm in uncharted waters here. Marcus is… he made me feel things that I have never felt before. It happened so fast. I'm excited, and I'm terrified. I don't know what I'm doing here."

Sidney gave her a quick hug. "It's okay, kiddo; you're just in love. Don't worry, Marcus is a good guy. After all, he is my twin. Why wouldn't he love you?"

"Hold on, Sidney. Let's not move too fast here."

"Okay, but I've been watching, and there's enough electricity between the two of you to light up a small town. Seriously, Steph, he would be good for you. Give him a chance."

"Okay, Sidney, we'll see what happens. He might just ignore me after he thinks about last night."

"I doubt that, sugar."

Marcus, Tate and Kevin walked in the kitchen, heading for the coffee pot on their way to work. Marcus said good morning and then turned to Stephanie and said good morning before heading out the door with his brothers. Stephanie blushed and dropped her head. Sidney said with a smile as she left to check on her grandmother, "Yep, a small town."

Chapter Thirteen

J.P. sat sipping a root beer at the Cove Restaurant, waiting for Marcus. He was a little surprised when Marcus asked if he had time for lunch at the Cove. The last time they had shared a meal there J.P. had invited him and had told him he had found his "forever girl." He had smiled to himself as Marcus went down a mental list of girls, canceling out each one of them. Then throwing up his hands, Marcus had said, "I don't know who it could be. The only girl you hang around is Sidney." With a shocked look on his face he asked, "Dude, you're crushing on my sister?"

J.P. had answered with a straight face, "I'm not crushing; I care about her. I've tried not to care, but I do, and I want to tell her, but I want it to be okay with you."

"So you're asking my permission to date my sister?"

"I guess I am."

"Does Sidney feel the same way?"

"I don't know. I want to talk with her, but I wanted to talk with you first."

Marcus had then sat back in his chair and said, "We have been friends a long time, and I trust you not to hurt her. If she feels the same way, it's okay with me."

J.P. was smiling as Marcus joined him at the table.

"Thanks for coming, J.P."

"No problem. Who's paying?"

Marcus replied, "I got this one."

"Okay, who's the lady?"

"Sidney's girlfriend, Stephanie. I like her; I really like her."

"Marcus, Sidney's been home for what, three weeks?"

"Dude, I know, and she's not even my type. She's white."

J.P. laughed out loud, "White? You mean white like me? Wow, you got it bad, dude."

"I know. One minute I'm minding my own business. The next minute I'm trying to breathe because she's in the room. She's got me thinking about forever. Me! Can you believe it?"

J.P. said with a grin, "Yeah, dude, its official, you're done. How the mighty have fallen?"

"J.P., I really like her. She's different, and I want to see if it can lead to something more."

"Well, let's pray about it and see what God has in store for you. She is saved, isn't she?"

"Yes, she is."

"When can I meet your Stephanie? What's her last name?"

"Uh… Uh… I don't know yet."

Grinning, J.P. said, "Dude, you're crushing on a girl, and you don't even know her name? Yeah, you got it bad, really bad."

Marcus, looking embarrassed and a little frustrated, said, "Enough of this, what's happening with Grams' account? Were you able to find out anything?"

Allowing him to change the subject, J.P. said, "I looked over her account history back to when we were in high school, and I found a foreclosure notice in her file. Do you remember anything about it?"

"No, I don't. In fact, I can remember Grams talking about how the Lord always made a way for our finances. I can ask her, but I'm pretty sure she would have told us about it."

"It's worth checking out. Can you talk with Grams? I think I'll stop by the bank and talk with Mrs. Fields in collections and see if she can remember anything about it. Something doesn't seem right with this."

As they were eating lunch, Marcus asked, "How's the Phoenix deal coming?"

"Great. Their modifications are really creative. They want their company name added to any initiatives that they bring to TCHD Crew. They even sent a proposed logo, and when discussions concerning their initiatives occur, they would like to be invited as guests to the board meetings. Our attorneys have reviewed the contract and given us the okay to move forward. I've already emailed Ms. Reed, letting her know we've accepted their modifications and are ready to sign the merger contract."

Marcus smiled and said, "I feel really good about this and think it's a good move for us."

"Me, too." J.P. said, grinning, "You know Ms. Reed's first name is Stephanie. Could she be your Stephanie? She's white and pretty."

"Not likely; this is Sidney's friend."

"Well, my friend, you need to find out that minor detail. Do you want me to ask her for you?"

"No! I do not. I can handle this. Have you tried talking with Sidney again?"

"I've tried, but she's avoiding me like the plague. I saw her in church, but she left before I could speak with her. I have to find out why she left. I wish we could just talk and clear this thing up."

"J.P., what happened to make you stop talking to me about Sidney? What made you give up on her?"

"She gave up on me. My dad showed me a magazine with her and some guy who she was dating. She gave up on me."

Marcus, staring at J.P., asked, "What guy? What are you talking about?"

J.P. bowed his head, took a deep breath and told Marcus about the argument he had with his father, how his father had said that Sidney never wanted to be with him and never felt the same way he felt about her. His father said she didn't care enough to say goodbye, and that she had found what she wanted. Then he handed J.P. a magazine showing Sidney with a guy. "When I read it I, realized she had moved on. She gave up on me," J.P. said, then fell silent as he looked up at Marcus.

Marcus could see the hurt that his friend was trying so hard to hide.

"J.P., Sidney wasn't dating that guy. He was her roommate's boyfriend, and she helped him get into the internship program."

"Marcus, are you sure?" Hope began to flare up in J.P.'s heart.

"J.P., why didn't you just ask me? I would have told you."

"I don't know; it was just easier not to feel at all, so I shut her out, and you, too. I'm sorry."

"It's okay; I'm just sorry it's taken this long to clear that up. What now?"

"I have to find out why she left, and how to get her back in my life."

They sat quietly, pondering over what to do next while they finished their meal. J.P. sat back in his chair and looked at Marcus, who, noticing him staring looked back with a raised eyebrow and said, "What?"

J.P. looked down at his empty plate, embarrassed, but then looked Marcus in the eyes with determination and said, "You know we have the basketball fund raiser coming up?"

"Yeah, we always volunteer for that, so?"

"So, this year they've changed from teams of two to teams of three..."

Realizing what J.P. was asking, Marcus started grinning and said, "Dude, you want me to fix you up with my sister?

"Marcus, she's avoiding me. I don't know why, and I need to talk with her."

Marcus' expression grew serious, "Okay, J.P., I'll talk with Grams and see if she can get Sidney to volunteer. This is one of Grams' largest church fundraisers, and I'm sure Sidney will want to help out. We can get her there, but after that…"

"Thanks, Marcus," J.P. said feeling some heaviness lift off his chest. He sent a silent prayer up to God. *Father, please show me the way. Forgive me for losing faith in Sidney and in You. Show me how to reach her now.*

≈≈≈

Saturday morning couldn't come fast enough for J.P. ever since Marcus told him that Sidney had agreed to volunteer and would be there on Saturday. He had been on pins and needles; his emotions were all over the place. He was so excited, and so afraid. He didn't know what he would say to her. By Friday night he officially declared himself a wreck and did the only thing that made sense. He went in his bedroom, fell on his knees and sought God for direction. *Father, you know how much I love Sidney. I have tried not to love her, but I can't help it. I believe she is the only one for me. I don't know what happened to cause her to leave. She said it wasn't me, but now she's avoiding me. When I see her tomorrow, please give us an opportunity to talk, and Father, if it be Your will, let her give me, give us another chance.* After praying, J.P. just sat

114

there while peace flowed into his body. He lifted his eyes to the heavens and said, *Thank you, Father.*

≈≈≈

Sidney told herself that she was ready; she knew she would see J.P. today. She had even rehearsed several scenarios of what she would say and do to get through the day without a repeat of their last encounter. If anyone else had asked her to volunteer, she would have said no, but she couldn't say no to Grams; she had to play today. The good news was that she knew J.P. would be playing with Marcus, so the worst that could happen would be that she would play against them. Since she had not played in a while she anticipated a quick loss. Then she could go home.

Sidney walked into the high school gym and signed in, picked up her team number and was told to meet her team in the left corner of the home team basket. She smiled as she looked at her number "5." It was her favorite number, and she considered it a good sign until she walked over to the corner and saw that J.P. and Marcus were wearing the number "5" too. She stopped and just stared.

Marcus walked over to her and said, "Hey, Ney, you ready to play?"

"Marcus what is going on? Why are we on the same team?"

"Oh, they changed from the two-player team to three-player teams this year." Looking at the despair on his sister's face, Marcus asked, "Are you okay? You don't have to play if you don't want to."

"No, I'll be alright; it's just a game, right?"

Marcus leaned in close and lowered his voice so no one else could hear and said, "Sidney, I know you still care for J.P. I think you two need to talk and clear the air. You can't avoid him forever."

Releasing a breath that she didn't know she was holding, Sidney said, "Okay, you're right. We do need to talk; maybe it's time."

Marcus gives her a big hug and said, "I love you, Ney."

Hugging him tight, she whispered, "I love you too, Marc."

≈≈≈

J.P. watched Sidney and Marcus talk from across the room. When he saw the distress on her face he felt pain slice through his heart, knowing she was stressing because of him. He closed his eyes and lifted a silent prayer, *Father, please, I don't want to hurt her. Please show me what to do.* When he opened his eyes, he was looking into Sidney's honey brown eyes.

"Hi, J.P. I guess we're teammates today."

"I guess so. Are you okay with this, Sidney? I can switch with someone if you don't want to play with me."

"No, it's okay. Maybe we can talk later if it's okay with you?"

Smiling, J.P. said, "I would like that, but for now lets play ball. You can play ball, right?"

"Yea, I play a little with my brothers," replied, Sidney, repeating what she told him the day they first met in elementary school.

The whistle blew and the games began. For the next four hours they played basketball and J.P. loved every minute of it. He was transported back in time as their rhythm returned, and he could sense where Sidney was on the court. He watched as Marcus and Sidney played off each other. He remembered longing for the rhythm they'd shared as kids, and was amazed that he was now sharing it even for a brief moment in time. J.P. drank in every nuance about Sidney, every facial expression, every laugh, everything, and stored them away, counting them as precious.

Too soon the games were over. J.P. was exhausted, but a big part of him wanted the game to never end. As Marcus and J.P. walked to the showers, Marcus said, "Why don't you shower first so you can spend some time with Sidney while I get changed?"

J.P. smiled and grabbed his clothes and headed for the showers.

Sidney waited for Marcus in the break room after the game, thinking how much fun she had with J.P. and Marcus. She couldn't help smiling at how well they played together, how carefree she felt playing with her guys. She chastened herself for claiming J.P. as hers; after all, the man was married. She reminded herself that she and J.P. could be friends and nothing more. Letting that thought settle in only made the dull ache in her heart more noticeable.

"Hi, Sidney," J.P. said as he sat down across from her at the table. "Did you enjoy the game?"

"Yes, I did. I was just thinking about how much fun it was. I'm just sorry Grams couldn't be here; she loves cheering for all the teams," Sidney responded, smiling at the memory.

J.P. gave a little laugh and said, "Remember the time Grams thought the referee was making bad calls?"

His laughter grew as Sidney giggled, "Yeah, she was so mad, I don't think she was even aware that she was standing on the court yelling at the referee. Uncle Ben had to get her off the court."

They both cracked up laughing at how Grams was led away, shouting that the ref needed glasses.

Half an hour later, they were still talking about shared memories, movies, books, food and, of course, basketball. Sidney sat back with a big smile on her face, thinking, *wow, this feels so good. It has been so long since I've spent time with my best friend.*

Then the mood changed, J.P. was still smiling, but his eyes grew intense, as if he were trying to search out answers to questions that only Sidney could answer. He leaned forward and covered her right hand with his and said, "Sidney, we need to talk, really talk. I know you said that I wasn't the reason you left, but I need to know why. We were best friends, more than friends, and then you left without saying anything. I don't understand why, and as much as I tell myself it doesn't matter, it does."

Sidney found it extremely hard to concentrate when J.P. was touching her hand. They were connected from the moment they touched. She was amazed that the connection was still there. Why did it feel so right to have him hold her hand? Pulling away before she gave in to the sweet sensation, Sidney said, "I'm sorry, you deserve an explanation, and I will give it to you, but I just need to talk with Grams before I tell you what happened. I plan to talk with her tonight, so maybe we can talk after that."

J.P. smiled and asked, "Have dinner with me?" After a long pause with no response from Sidney, he said, "Okay, how about we meet after church at the picnic table?"

Sidney smiled and said, "Great, I can do that, tomorrow after church."

"Hey, Sidney, you ready?" Marcus asked as he walked into the break room.

"Oh, wow! I told Stephanie that I shouldn't be more than a couple of hours. It's six hours later; I never expected to win so many games today. I need to get home and give Stephanie a break." Turning to J.P., she gave him a big smile and said, "I'll see you tomorrow."

J.P. just stood there with big grin on his face and said, "Yes, tomorrow, after church."

He couldn't wipe that stupid grin off his face to save his life; he had just had the best 30 minutes of his life, being with Sidney. Tomorrow she would tell him what happened to make her leave him, and if he read her right, she still might have feelings for him. Heading for his car, J.P. sent a prayer of thanksgiving to God. *Father, thank you so much for being with Sidney and me and giving us this time to share and talk. Thank you*!

"J.P., J.P.!" Melinda walked over to him in her three-inch heels. "There you are."

"Melinda. . . what are you doing here?"

"I ran into you father at the bank and he told me that you were playing a basketball game for charity today, so I decided to come cheer for you."

"Oh, thanks. You really didn't have to do that."

"Well the game was over by the time I got here, but since I'm here, maybe we can get some dinner?" Melinda flashed those big, blue eyes at him again.

"Sorry, I'm heading back to the office; I have some work to do." J.P. opened the truck door to get in.

Melinda asked, "Who was that girl you were talking to in the break room?"

"She was a friend from school. I have to run, Melinda. Take care."

As Melinda walked to her car, nursing her bruised ego, she decided she would talk with John, J.P.'s father, about this friend from school. She found that she was unnerved that J.P. had looked at that black girl with hopeful desire and furious that he had never looked at her that way. *Hmm, friend from school or an obstacle in my way.*

Well, little friend from school, I have come too far to allow you to get in my way.

Chapter Fourteen

Sidney knocked softly on Grams' bedroom door before opening it to peek in. She saw Grams sleeping like a baby and didn't have the heart to wake her up to talk about her finances. Telling herself she would get up early to talk with Grams before going to church, Sidney headed to her room. Stopping by Stephanie's bedroom to thank her for taking care of Grams, she found her room empty and smiled as she hoped that Stephanie was spending time with Marcus. Sidney felt that Stephanie was almost in love with her brother and she was thrilled about it. She loved Stephanie and Marcus and knew they would be good for each other. It would only be a matter of time before they came to realize what they really wanted. She just had to wait and pray.

≈≈≈

Marcus found Stephanie on the back porch, "Hi Steph, can I join you?"

"Sure, how was the game?" Stephanie asked, smiling.

"It was great; we won three games before losing in the finals. It was a lot of fun. I'm sorry you missed it."

"Me too, but I had a great time with Grams. I love spending time with her, and she really knows how to spoil me. I loved every minute of it."

"I know how you feel. All my friends used to follow me home to hang out with Grams. They said it was her cooking, but I knew they felt special with Grams. She knew just how to reach them and draw them out. My college buddies still come by on holidays just to see her. I can't tell you how many of them bring their girlfriends by for Grams' approval. Grams says it's her gift from God." Changing the subject, Marcus asked, "Hey, do you play basketball?"

"Are you kidding me? Sidney Weston is my best friend. Do I play basketball? Yes, I can play a little bit." She gave Marcus a sly smile.

"Well, I guess we'll have to see how much is a little bit. Come on, best two out of three, and I'll even give you a six point advantage."

"So the game is 20 points, and I get a six point advantage. Is that right?

Marcus gave her a dubious look and said, "Why do I get the feeling I'm being set up? Okay, let's go."

Stephanie giggled as they walked to the basketball court and played two games, with Marcus winning both by only a couple of points. Laughing as they walked off the court. Marcus said, "The golden girl is beautiful and talented; Sidney has taught you well. And by the way, no more six point advantage for you."

Stephanie smiled and said, "Sorry, I should have told you. Whenever we were frustrated or needed a stress break, Sidney and I played basketball. I never really played sports until I met her. Now I play a few sports and do a little rock climbing. I actually love being in shape."

Marcus walked her to the foot of the stairs leading to her room and asked, "So would you like to go running with me in the morning?"

"What time?"

"If we run at 6:00 a.m., I can take you out for breakfast at 7:30 a.m.?"

"Okay, I'd like that."

"Great! I'll meet you at 6:00 a.m. in the backyard," Marcus said as he leaned in and kissed her on the cheek and whispered, "Goodnight, Steph."

Pulse racing, Stephanie said, "Goodnight, Marcus."

Marcus stood at the bottom of the stairs until he heard Stephanie's door close before heading to his room in the basement, smiling about his morning run with Stephanie.

≈≈≈

After church Sidney headed to the picnic table behind the building. Service was great, but it took great effort to stay focused on the message, which was to be sober and vigilant because your enemy the devil walks around like a roaring lion, seeking who he can destroy. As she approached the table, she saw that someone was already there, a beautiful, tall, blonde woman with big, blue eyes. As Sidney turned to leave, the woman called out to her, "You must be Sidney Weston."

"Yes, I am. Do I know you?"

"No, you don't, but you know my husband, J.P. Carter, and I would appreciate it if you would stop chasing him like a harlot."

Sidney's world stopped. She just stared, unable to say a word as tears streamed down her cheeks. She couldn't move, couldn't get out of the line of fire as this woman hurled insult after insult at her.

Melinda could see that she had won. She had effectively removed this obstacle to her plans, but she wanted to humiliate her, to bring this black girl to her knees, so she kept going, asking Sidney who did she think she was chasing a married man, and a white man at that. "Do you really think he could ever love you?" she screamed.

"Melinda, what are you doing?!"

Melinda turned to see J.P. staring at her with rage in his eyes.

J.P. couldn't believe what he was hearing; Melinda was screaming at Sidney, accusing her of chasing a married man. The hurt he saw in Sidney's eyes cut through him and nearly buckled his knees. He went to her. "Sidney, I am so sorry. Are you okay?"

Backing up, Sidney wiped the tears overflowing from her eyes, saying, "I'm sorry, I'm so sorry." Turning, she ran as if the hounds from hell were chasing her.

J.P. started after Sidney, but was pulled up short by Melinda grabbing his arm. He stared at the hand that kept him from leaving and realized that he needed to deal with Melinda here and now.

"Melinda, what have you done?"

"J.P. let her go. It's all for the better. Besides you and I …"

"There is no, I repeat no 'you and I.' I don't know what you were thinking or where you got the idea that I was ever interested in you, but I am not, and I have never, ever been interested in a relationship with you. Now, if you continue to pursue this crazy idea, I will have a restraining order placed on you, and I will contact a good friend of mine, who is also a reporter and share an interesting story of a socialite turned stalker." J.P. stated each threat with steel determination, watching as Melinda's face registered defeat, then surprise, then shock.

"I thought we had something special. I see that I was mistaken. You will not have to worry about me approaching you again." Then she lifted her head and squared her shoulders and walked away.

J.P. watched her walk away and pulled out his cell phone and called Sidney. No answer. He texted her. No response. The feeling of dread was settling in his stomach. Not knowing what else to do, he called Marcus.

"What did you do to my sister?! She's in her room crying her eyes out. She won't let anyone in, not even Stephanie. J.P. what happened?!" Marcus yelled at him.

"Marcus, I don't know. We were supposed to meet and talk, but when I got here, Melinda was here screaming at her. I stopped it, but Sidney ran away. I know she's hurt but I don't know what to do."

Marcus sounded puzzled, "What does Melinda have to do with this?"

"I don't know. Lately she has been showing up. She was at my dad's party and she came to the basketball game yesterday, now at church. She said she thought we had something special. Marcus, you know that I've never been interested in Melinda."

"That I do know. So what's really happening?"

"I know my dad has been trying to fix me up with Melinda."

"Why were you late for church today?"

"My dad called and told me he had an emergency. He needed me to check on some safety deposits, something about the drop box being tampered with. So I went in and checked the deposits and locked them in the safe. There wasn't anything out of the ordinary, but I wanted to secure the deposits. It took me away from service and I couldn't get there until after church."

Marcus asked another question, "How did Melinda know about the game?"

"She said she ran into dad at the bank and he told her I was playing for charity so she came to cheer me on." J.P. continued on, "So dad is still trying to set me up with Melinda. Marcus, Sidney was going to tell me why she left."

Marcus let out a long breath, "Now it makes more sense. I don't know what they told her, but I have never seen her like this."

"Marcus, can I come see her, please."

Marcus said, "I don't think that's a good idea, J.P. She's hurting too much. I can feel it. Let's pray and ask God to minister to her and expose every lie that's been spoken to her."

Over the phone J.P. and Marcus lifted their voices in prayer for Sidney, asking for God to heal the hurt that she was experiencing and to bring the truth to light. J.P. asked for patience to wait while God worked with Sidney and for wisdom in finding out why she left Resting Place. After they prayed, J.P. climbed into his truck and headed home.

≈≈≈

Sidney rubbed her eyes, and pushed her hair out of her face. She lay on her bed looking up at the dark ceiling, wondering how she got to this place. She had been praying, asking for forgiveness ever since she ran away from J.P. and his wife. She kept hearing Melinda scream at her about chasing a married man. Her words were like daggers in Sidney's heart. She wasn't chasing J.P., was she? Yet, if she was honest with herself, she knew her feelings were far deeper than friendship. The feelings of guilt at that moment were so great and her emotions so raw, she couldn't talk with anyone about it, not yet. She knew eventually she would have to explain what had happened that caused her to shut herself in her room and cry, but for now she needed to pray. She needed to get her emotions under control and deal with the inappropriate feelings she had toward J.P.

As Sidney slid off the bed onto her knees, she bowed her head in prayer, crying out to God about the events of the day, about her love for J.P., and about what to do next. One hour later, knees hurting, Sidney got up, with the Scripture whispering in her mind. "Trust in the Lord with all your heart and lean not to your own understanding..." *Well, God, I don't understand, but I do feel better; I want to bring You glory and not shame. I feel like I brought You shame today.* "Trust in the Lord with all your heart and lean not to your own understanding..." *Okay, I trust You. I don't understand and I don't know what you are doing, but I do trust You.* Sidney headed for the shower, and passing her desk, she saw the Phoenix paperwork and decided that she would read over it before going to bed. *Today was bad, really bad, but if she kept moving, eventually she would be okay. Right,*

God? "Trust in the Lord with all your heart and lean not to your own understanding…"

≈≈≈

On the drive home, J.P.'s mind was full, thinking about everything that had happened and how it all tied back to his father. He wondered if what happened today could also have something to do with why Sidney left. He felt the weight of the events of the day and was frustrated that he couldn't see Sidney, and didn't know how to ease her pain. J.P. headed straight for his room and fell on his face and prayed for Sidney, crying out to God to comfort her and give her peace. Afterwards he sat on the floor and just listened for what to do next. Then, realizing the answers that he sought might be in the past, J.P. sat staring at a box of items that Sidney had given him over the years. He usually kept it in the back of his closet, but had pulled it out since Sidney's return. As he opened the box, he smiled as sweet memories flooded his mind. He picked up each item, holding it, studying it, and putting it back in its place.

One of the last items J.P. picked out was the dog tag Sidney had given him for his seventeenth birthday. Once he had become a Christian, he was very serious about being a man of God. He so wanted to be like his Heavenly Father and not his earthly father. J.P. had talked a lot with Sidney concerning his dad, about how he never wanted to be like him. When J.P. accepted Christ as his Lord and Savior and found out more about God, he was determined to be a man of God. It meant a lot to him that Sidney had bought the dog tag that had "Man Of God" inscribed on it for his birthday. His love for her grew that night even before their first kiss, and after that kiss, his heart was lost to her forever. As he rubbed the dog tag between his fingers, he allowed his mind to drift back to their Senior Prom, the last time he was with Sidney.

J.P. remembered talking with his dad before leaving to pick up Sidney. His dad asked if he had enough money and who was the lucky girl. When J.P. said Sidney, he remembered his dad was really upset and mumbled something. J.P. was so nervous that he didn't pay attention to what his dad was talking about. This was his first official date with Sidney and he wanted it to be perfect. They had been studying for finals that week and had agreed not to see each other until after finals were over. He had done well on his exams, and according to Sidney's last e-mail, so had she. That night they could relax and just spend time together. That night he would tell her how he felt, that he loved her, and see if she loved him.

Tonight they would plan their future. He was so excited, he couldn't wait.

≈≈≈

When J.P. saw Sidney coming down the stairs he could only stare. He was talking with Grams, Marcus and Marcus' date, and in the middle of a sentence he forgot what he was saying. His words disappeared as his eyes focused on Sidney. She was so beautiful; her hair was loose around her shoulders, framing her pecan brown face. The pale blue dress she wore emphasized her tiny waistline. She looked amazing. "Wow, you look great!"

Sidney blushed and said, "Thanks." Grams stepped in with her camera, and after a couple dozen pictures, they were on their way.

That night in J.P.'s mind was magical. He couldn't take his eyes off Sidney; the rest of the world disappeared, and as they slow danced while he held her in his arms, breathing in the faint scent of coconut, he whispered, "I love you, Sidney."

He heard her whisper back, "I love you, too, J.P." When the music ended, he escorted her outside, held her close and shared tender kisses. They held each other and planned their summer, how they would see each other when J.P. left for college. Sidney was planning to attend a local college, so they talked about him making weekend visits and spending their breaks together.

J.P. remembered Sidney being really worried about his dad finding out about them. She didn't want him to tell his dad for fear that he would break them up. He didn't like the idea of keeping his relationship with Sidney a secret from his dad or anyone else, but seeing her concern and the fear in her eyes caused him to agree not to tell his dad. Thinking back, J.P. remembered that his dad already knew that he was out on a date with her. *Oh Sidney, what happened?* He reached for the phone and texted Marcus, checking on Sidney, and letting Marcus know that he would be late getting to the office; he was going to stop by the bank. As J.P. drifted off to sleep, he prayed, "Father guide me; show me what I can't see."

≈≈≈

J.P. was waiting in the parking lot of Carter Savings and Loans Bank, when Mrs. Fields arrived to work at 7:00 a.m. sharp, which had been her habit for over twenty years. "Good morning, Mrs. Fields."

"Good morning, J.P. You're up early this morning. What can I do for you?"

"I'm doing research on some foreclosures and wanted to talk with you before you got too busy."

"Well, I can certainty help with that, but I can't give you any personal information."

"Okay, I have a few property addresses I want information on."

As they walked to her office making small talk, J.P. gave Mrs. Fields Grams' address plus three others that were on the same street. Jotting down the addresses, she turned on her computer and checked each property's account.

"Only one out of the four has had a foreclosure notice. Let me pull that file." Mrs. Fields left the room briefly and came back with a folder in hand. "Oh, I remember this one. I thought is sounded familiar. I was home sick when this one happened."

Curious, J.P. said, "What happened?"

"Well, I had been feeling badly that whole week, tired, body aches, sore throat, but I pushed myself because it was the end of the month, and we were closing out the books. By Friday I was dragging, and all I wanted to do was get in the bed. I promised myself that I would spend the weekend in bed and nurse that cold. Around 9:00 p.m. Friday night, your dad gave me a call and woke me up, telling me he needed me to process some foreclosure paperwork on that property. I asked him what was the hurry because the owner wasn't 30 days past due. You know how your dad gets when he doesn't want to answer a direct question? He kept right on talking, telling me he wanted that paperwork on his desk by 9:00 a.m. the next day, Saturday. I told him that I would be in early on Saturday to get it done.

"I guess he felt bad about having me work on the weekend sick, because he gave me that Monday off. As it turned out, when I came in on Tuesday, he told me to cancel the paperwork. I can pull up more property information for you."

J.P. listened to Mrs. Fields, trying to take in all the information. His dad did this; he made Sidney leave by threatening to foreclose on Grams' mortgage. With more calm than he felt, he said, "Thanks, Mrs. Fields. That won't be necessary. I have enough information."

On the drive back to his office, J.P.'s anger grew to the point of rage. His dad had played him well; he had removed Sidney and tried replacing her with many other women, and currently with Melinda. He just didn't count on J.P. really loving Sidney. He thought about the picture and the article, how his dad had lied and tried to destroy any future J.P. had with Sidney. And yesterday with Melinda, again, his dad was trying to get rid of Sidney. *Well, I won't let her leave me again. I can't let her go.* J.P. prayed, "Lord help me; I am so angry with my dad that I don't know what I would do if I saw him right now."

Chapter Fifteen

J.P. marched into his office, calling over his shoulder to Carrie, his receptionist, "Get Marcus now."

A few minutes later Marcus walked into J.P.'s office without knocking, saying, "What happened?"

"It was my dad all along. He ran Sidney away."

Taking in what J.P. was telling him, Marcus spoke through clenched teeth. "How?"

"He threatened to foreclose on Grams' house."

As understanding dawned on him, Marcus said, "Now, it makes sense why Sidney worked a full-time job and went to school full time. She sent almost all of her paychecks to Grams with a note to pay the mortgage."

J.P. stared at Marcus and said, "She was trying to pay it off so she could come back home. Her last e-mail makes sense now. She wanted me to wait for her, but why didn't she come back?"

"Grams told me that Sidney was coming home about three years after she left, right around the time when you were supposed to be engaged."

J.P. snorted, "I know dad had something to do with that. Do you think she heard about it?"

Marcus nodded, "Afraid so; that was big news around here, and it was on the Help Desk e-mail. I know she got it, and that's why she didn't come home. She even stopped talking with me for a while then."

J.P.'s anger grew as he realized the depth of his father's deception. Then in a startled voice he said, "She must think I'm still engaged or married to Melinda. No wonder she ran from me! What must she think of me?! Marcus, I've got to see her! I have to explain. How could my father do this to me?"

Marcus looked at his watch and said, "I'm sorry, J.P., but the Phoenix owners will be here in a little over an hour. We have to meet with them; we both have to be here to sign the merger paperwork."

"Okay, okay. I'll leave as soon as the meeting is over."

Marcus watched J.P. pace back and forth like a caged lion, furious. He had never seen J.P. so upset and knew that nothing good would come from acting on the rage that was brewing in his friend. Taking a deep breath and calming his own emotions, Marcus said, "Right now we need to pray and seek the Lord's help with this. We can't take matters into our own hands; we need God's help and direction."

J.P. stared at Marcus for a few minutes, struggling to gain control over the anger within. Closing his eyes and bowing his head, he spoke in a barely audible voice, "Okay." They joined hands and prayed first Marcus, then J.P. As he finished praying, calm came over J.P. as if the Lord had whispered peace to his spirit, and then began giving him a plan. J.P. smiled and said, "I have a lot of work to do before our meeting with Phoenix. I have some calls to make."

Marcus looked at him and asked, "You okay?"

"Yes, finally, I am okay. The Lord has just shown me how to handle this thing with Sidney, but I don't have a lot of time to do it. Can you prepare for the Phoenix meeting? I need to call my attorney."

Marcus gave a thoughtful smile and said, "Sure, no problem."

One hour later J.P. breathed a sigh of relief and thanked God for His goodness and His peace; then he asked for wisdom on how to reach Sidney.

Marcus stuck his head in the office a few minutes before the meeting. "Are you ready?"

Picking up the phone, J.P. said, "Yeah, I'm expecting a fax. Give me a minute to let Carrie know that I need her to bring it to me as soon as it arrives... Okay, that's done. I'm ready."

"Good. They 're waiting in the conference room." As they walked out of J.P.'s office, they heard the fax machine.

≈≈≈

Sidney and Stephanie arrived at 8:50 a.m. for their 9:00 a.m. appointment and were escorted by a young woman to a conference room. They were informed that the President and Vice-President would join them shortly. Stephanie turned to Sidney, so excited that she could hardly sit still, "You're going to like these people, Sidney; they are not like Bolen IT executives. They're all around our age, and they really wanted to hear about what we had to offer. I just know this is a good move for us."

"I think so too, Steph, and I already like them on paper. If I haven't told you, Steph, you have done an amazing job putting this together. Thank you for taking the whole load while I stayed with Grams. You have done an impressive job, partner."

Reaching over to give Sidney a hug, Stephanie whispered in her ear, "That's what partners do; they take care of each other. Thank you, for trusting me with a partnership. I love you, Sidney."

"I love you too, Steph."

Both women turned when the conference room door opened to see J.P. and Marcus there. J.P. and Marcus stopped short of entering the room when they saw Sidney and Stephanie sitting at the table with shocked looks on their faces. J.P. and Marcus looked at each other, and then J.P. began to smile and said under his breath, *Thank You, Lord.* He realized that God had answered his prayer in providing a way for him to talk with Sidney, and also revealing Stephanie's last name to Marcus.

Sidney's mind froze, as she asked herself, *What is J.P. doing here?* She was not prepared for this. Her next thought was; I *have to get out of here.* J.P., predicting her thoughts, moved in front of the door, blocking her exit, then said in a calm voice, "Marcus, could you take Ms. Reed out for a late breakfast? I need to talk with Sidney."

Marcus walked over to Stephanie, smiled, closing the space between them and whispered, "J.P. and Sidney need to talk."

Realizing that John Carter was J.P., Stephanie stared in shock. Regaining her composure, she grabbed Marcus' arm and asked, "Is he married?"

"No, he's not, and they have a lot to clear up."

Smiling, Stephanie got up, gave Sidney a hug, and said, "Trust God, Sidney; He won't make you ashamed." Stephanie and Marcus headed out the conference room.

Marcus, holding Stephanie's hand, pulled her close and casually said, "Reed, so that's your last name."

"You didn't know?"

Marcus couldn't stop smiling as he said, "No, I didn't, but I will rectify that right now. So what's your favorite color?" Marcus asked as he closed the conference room door behind them.

≈≈≈

Sidney steeled herself, praying for a good outcome. They needed this partnership, but she didn't know how she would work so close to J.P. Maybe Stephanie could take the lead, and she could remain in the background. *Lord help me, I don't know what to do.* Taking a deep breath she said, "J.P., I didn't know that TCHD was your company. We can…"

"Our company," J.P. said softly, cutting her off.

Sidney started again, "We can modify…"

Shaking his head with a smile, stopping her from talking, J.P. said, "Sidney, TCHD is part yours; you have stock in this company. TCHD is the Technology Club Help Desk, our class project. You named the project, I just shortened the name to TCHD, so technically you named this company and Marcus, you and I own it. Your earnings have gone into an account that I set up for you when we started the company." J.P. walked over to her, holding her gaze until they were face to face.

Sidney, more confused than ever, wanted to run, to escape, but her feet refused to move.

"Sidney, you told me that you loved me, and that nothing would ever change that and you asked me to wait for you. So do you still love me?"

His words pierced her heart; she turned away from the intense look in his liquid brown eyes.

"I can't do this," she said as she turned away from him.

He reached for her and turned her around to face him. "Sidney, I know why you left. I know about the mortgage. I know what my dad did." He pulled her into his arms, and he felt her stiffen. Then she began to struggle to get free.

"J.P. let me go."

"No, I can't. I can't let you go again, not again, never again. Sidney, I'm not married, and I'm not engaged. That was all a part of my dad's plan to keep us apart. I've never been engaged to Melinda or anyone else."

As J.P.'s words began to sink in, understanding what he said, Sidney's heart opened, and hope filled her being. She began to relax in his arms. "You're not married or engaged?"

"No. The woman I wanted to marry left me an e-mail that said she loved me so much and nothing would ever change that, and she asked me to wait for her. I don't have the heart for anyone else. I gave my heart to her."

Tears of joy ran down Sidney's face. J.P. wiped them away with the pad of his thumb, saying, "Do you still mean it, Sidney? Do you still love me? Because, I have never stopped loving you."

"J.P., I love you so much. I tried not to, but I couldn't stop loving you."

J.P. looked into Sidney's eyes, allowing her to see all the love he held for her alone. Then moving closer, he claimed her lips ever so softly. Her kiss was so sweet and so right; it felt like coming home. When they ended the kiss, J.P. asked, "Will you marry me, Sidney?" He watched the emotions that crossed her face: joy, wonder, then concern and fear.

"What about your dad? J.P., he never wanted us together. What about Grams' house? The bank still owns it. I love you so much, but I can't see Grams lose her home."

J.P. reached in his jacket pocket and pulled out some folded papers he had gotten from Carrie before walking into the meeting. He handed them to Sidney, saying. "Sidney, I love Grams as if she were my own mother. I won't allow her or you to live in fear about losing her home, but before you look at that, I want to say I'm sorry for what happened with my dad. What he did hurt so many people, but I have seen to it that he can't hurt you or your family anymore." He leaned down and kissed her again and told her to open it.

She unfolded the paper and read it. "J.P., this is the deed to Grams' house, and it's marked paid in full. How did you do this?"

J.P. sat in one of the conference chairs, pulling Sidney onto his lap, not able to let her separate from him. Holding her in his arms, he said, "Before my mom passed, she held 51 percent of the stock in the bank, and some other investments dad didn't know about. Mom knew dad was cheating on her, so when she got sick she contacted her attorney to set up a trust fund for me that her attorney managed until I turned 21 years old.

I didn't know that my mom was very wealthy and that Carter Savings and Loans, originally named Resting Place Savings and Loans, were passed down through my mom's family. When they got married, dad talked her into changing the name of the bank. I believe mom had always regretted doing that."

J.P. stopped, held Sidney's left hand, kissing her fingers, and then asked again, "Sidney, will you marry me?"

"I love you so much! Yes, I will marry you!"

Just before he kissed her again, he asked, "Soon?"

After their kiss, Sidney said breathlessly, "Finish your story."

"Oh, yeah, when I turned 21 my mom's attorney contacted me for a meeting. Mom had left me a letter explaining that she didn't trust dad to handle my estate, and that she wanted me to use the money to pursue my dreams. She also told me that one day I would have to choose to continue to live under my dad's influence or choose to follow God. Shortly after my 21st birthday we used some of the money to start TCHD Crew Company. My dad never believed that the business would prosper, so he continued to deposit monthly funds in my bank account. I didn't need it because TCHD did so well we started creating satellite sites in remote areas to create jobs. So I put the money my dad gave into more investments."

J.P. stopped and looked at Sidney in wonder, and whispered, *Thank you, Father,* before continuing, "When I found out what dad had done, I was so... angry, I... didn't know what to do. Then Marcus and I prayed, and God showed me that I was in a position to remove the threat that my dad has held over your head all these years. So I called my attorney and told him that I wanted to pay off Grams' mortgage using the money I had invested. It was more than enough to cover the remaining balance. There is nothing that dad can do to you or Grams now."

"Thank you, J.P., thank you! I love you so much!"

Looking into Sidney's eyes, J.P. could see the love and longing that she had been hiding from him, and it took his breath away.

As he moved close to kiss her again, Sidney sent a silent prayer of thanks to God for guiding her home, restoring everything that had been taken away.

Epilogue

One month later Sidney woke up with a smile on her face as Stephanie rushed into her room. "Are you up? We have so much to do before the wedding. Sidney, I can't believe you're getting married today."

"Stephanie, I can't believe you're engaged to my brother. We're going to be sisters!" They hugged each other, wiping tears of joy from their eyes. Sidney said, "Okay, no more tears, even though they were happy ones."

Grams came in the room after a soft knock on the door, her arm still in a cast. "How are my girls?" Grams asked while giving them each a big hug and a kiss. "Okay, let's get a move on. The wedding is at 11:00 o'clock sharp, and we don't want to keep the groom or the best man waiting, do we, girls?"

They both said together, "No, ma'am," and burst into giggles and more tears of joy.

Grams got up to leave, but turned and asked, "Will Mr. Carter be joining us today?"

"No, Grams, he's really angry about me and J.P. and your mortgage. J.P. said he and his father will come to terms. He's praying about it."

"I will add him to my prayer list as well and trust God to move in his life. Well, ladies, get up and get moving. We have a wedding to attend!"

≈≈≈

J.P. and Marcus stood at the altar in black tuxes, waiting. They exchanged smiles speaking things in their hearts without words. They had stayed up talking until the early hours of the morning about the providence of God. J.P. realized that the deceptions of his father had worked out for his and Marcus' good.

Marcus marveled at how God's hand had placed Stephanie, his fiancée, in his life, realizing that it was because Sidney left that she met and became friends with Stephanie.

J.P.'s anger toward his father begin to disappear, now that he could see that what his dad meant for evil, God worked for their good. Looking around at everyone he loved, his heart was so full; he couldn't stop thanking God for blessing him with this family and with his soon-to-be wife, Sidney.

The music changed to the wedding march. Everyone stood, and there she was, moving toward him like a vision, a dream come true. J.P. couldn't take his eyes off Sidney, she was so beautiful. Kevin, Sidney's oldest brother, walked her to the altar, kissed Sidney on the cheek and gave J.P. a hug before taking his seat. As they turned to face their pastor, J.P. realized he had finally come to his place of rest, and he thanked God for bringing Sidney home to Resting Place.